Bad Ruck

Ruck Boys
Book 4

Maggie Alabaster

Chapter One

Chelsea

I DON'T KNOW HOW LONG I STOOD THERE, MY eyes locked on Ramsey's. I couldn't tear myself away from his gaze. They held a warning, I just didn't know what for.

Finally, I shook my head and broke the stare. "What did you—"

"Chelsea? What's wrong?" It was Atlas, holding a small brown dog, who came to stand in front of me. Blocking my line of sight.

I shook my head slowly, trying to clear it. "I don't know. Dallas isn't here. Ramsey said he left the stadium before him." My gaze found Atlas' face, and the worried furrow of his brow.

I didn't want to say the words out loud, so I whispered, "I have a bad feeling."

"Fuck." Atlas looked at Ramsey, then me. He handed the dog to one of the shelter staff and stalked over to Ramsey.

I hurried along behind, acutely aware the other guys were starting to notice something was going on.

"Chelsea said—" Atlas started.

Ramsey interrupted. "I know what she said. Let's not do this here."

"Where is he?" I asked. I tried to contain my fear, shove it down or away, but I failed miserably. If he did something to Dallas...

"What did you do?" Storm was beside my right elbow, face like thunder ready to strike. Or take a swing.

"Same question," Frost was beside him. He was slightly calmer, his expression more neutral, but his tone was no less accusing.

"What's going on?" Jay held a fluffy white cat and looked at all of us in confusion.

"That's what we're trying to find out," Atlas said. He raised his eyebrows at Ramsey.

Ramsey sighed. "I don't know where he is. He overheard Otis Skinner and I talking."

"What were you talking about?" I demanded. We were supposed to be able to trust him.

At this exact moment? I didn't. He was acting too squirrelly. Too suspicious as fuck.

My brother would say if it seems like he has something to hide, he probably does. Right before he chained them up and worked the truth loose from them.

Ramsey rubbed a hand over the back of his head, his mouth pressed in a frustrated line. "Can we talk about this somewhere else?" he asked through clenched teeth.

He glanced over to the camera crew, who were currently occupied with a couple of the other players. It wouldn't be long before they also realised something was going on. Something with the potential to be more newsworthy than a bunch of cute animals. If they started digging, a bad situation would turn to shit in a heartbeat.

We didn't need that kind of scrutiny. I certainly didn't.

"I think we're done here." Storm nodded at Jay to return the cat to the shelter staff, and eyed the team's PR person, as if daring them to say they weren't finished.

Fortunately for everyone, she nodded to indicate they got what they needed from the guys: advertising for the animal shelter in the hope more people would adopt the pets there.

Personally, I would have taken several animals home if I had room for them. Apparently I had a thing for collecting strays.

Keeping himself behind us, Storm herded us to the exit and out into the street.

"I'm not going to make a run for it," Ramsey said over his shoulder.

"Says you." Storm glared at him and waved us all over to a small park near the shelter. Little more than a patch of grass with a few trees and a couple of benches, it was private enough for now.

"Talk." Storm crossed his arms over his massive chest and glared at Ramsey. His narrowed, cold eyes, furrowed brow and turned down mouth would have intimidated a lot of people.

Apparently not Ferris Ramsey.

He lowered himself to the centre of a picnic bench, hands on either side of him, posture relaxed, as if he was discussing which dog he might adopt. Or maybe a cat. He seemed like a cat person to me. Secretive and cute but deadly.

"I've been trying to convince Otis Skinner I'm working with him. With full knowledge of those *we* work for. Skinner and I were making plans. Nothing any of you need to know about, but something I was going to fuck with later. Dallas overheard us. He made assumptions. I had to convince Otis he was working with us too."

My blood ran cold. "How?" What the hell had he done?

"By sending Dallas to give a message to a contact of mine. He shouldn't have taken this long." Ramsey dropped his head and shook it. Now he appeared rattled.

"Fuck," Storm growled. "If Otis wasn't fooled..."

"Dallas could be dead," I whispered.

I immediately regretted saying the words out loud. My heart thudded painfully.

I told myself I wouldn't cry, but I found my eyes damp anyway. He couldn't be dead. If he was, I'd... I'd be shattered.

The thought of losing any of my guys was a stab right through my soul. Had I told him that? Did I make him understand how much he meant to me? All I could think right now was that I'd left so many words unsaid. Too many.

Frost slipped an arm around my shoulders and gently pulled me to him. "There's probably some logical explanation. He might have gotten side-tracked by something perfectly innocent. Maybe he went to buy you a big box of chocolates. Or a new knife."

He sounded so certain. So convincing. I wanted to believe all of it, badly.

"You really think so?" I sniffed.

It was possible, I conceded that much, but was he right?

Honestly, I wished I believed he was. In reality, this was Dusk Bay. Dallas could easily be dead or missing, never to be seen again. Quietly disposing of corpses was something far too many people in this city were good at, including my brother. Making people disappear was an occupational necessity.

"I absolutely think so," Frost said, with unwavering conviction. "Dallas knows how much you like chocolate, and your period is due in a couple of days."

I turned my head to stare at him.

He smiled and shrugged. "We pay attention to these things. How else are we supposed to make sure you have everything you need?"

"That's sweet," I said. I should have known they were all over that.

"Exactly," Frost said. "Have you tried to call him?"

"A couple of times," I said. "It went to voicemail. I thought he might have been driving, but he..." I didn't know how to finish that sentence. Ultimately, I didn't need to. They all knew what the possibilities were.

"I'll try." Storm pulled out his phone and tapped the screen. He put the device to his ear and frowned. "Hey, Tex, where the fuck are you? Call me back." He ended the call and shoved his phone back into his pocket. "Voicemail."

"He might have his phone switched to silent," Jay suggested. "I always do, because the only people who call these days are scammers and telemarketers."

"Aren't those the same thing?" Frost asked.

"Close enough," Jay agreed. "Either way, I don't answer my phone unless I feel it ringing, and know the person. Even then, I have to be in the mood to talk to them."

"Dallas wouldn't ignore Chelsea," Frost said. "Unless he didn't hear his phone. It makes sense that he might have it turned off. Mine is off too."

"Mine too," Atlas said.

"I have to keep mine on in case of emergencies," I said. But I got it. I also didn't answer calls if I didn't know the number. At least, not if they weren't local. I had no reason to think anyone from Edinburgh would call me. Or Azerbaijan. I pulled out my own phone and sent off a couple of texts to Dallas.

Call me

Or text me back

I love you 🩶

With any luck, he'd see them. I hoped like hell he *could*. I wiped my eyes and put my phone away.

"Just to clear it up, you're not working with Otis Skinner?" Storm squinted at Ramsey.

"Absolutely not," Ramsey said, his mouth twisted to the side in disgust. "I reached out when he first joined the team, trying to figure out his angle. So far, he's kept me at arm's length. Today I was finally getting somewhere. He doesn't trust me, but he's starting to rely on me for information."

"Which you're not giving to him?" Storm's jaw worked, his annoyance clear.

"Just enough to make him think I'm reliable," Ramsey said, staring him down. "The names of a couple of contacts we already know are quietly working against us. Times and places of shipment arrivals. Nothing major. Nothing to indicate we have anything other than a professional relationship."

"He has no idea you're working for Daze?" I asked.

"He knows, but he thinks I'm disgruntled," Ramsey said. "That I'm looking for a bigger score."

"Are you?" Storm asked.

"I'm looking to stop him and Dominic King from getting a foothold in Dusk Bay." Ramsey tilted his head and looked back at Storm, his gaze unwavering. "It's not good for the city and it's not good for the team. We have enough people already vying for power, we don't need another one. Especially one as unscrupulous as Dominic King."

"How bad is he?" I asked. If he was unscrupulous compared to the other operators in the city, he must be terrible. That yardstick was extremely high.

"He's as ambitious as they come," Ramsey said. "At least as bad as the Fiorelli family were." Most of them were killed years ago, after trying to seize a bigger chunk of power. They would have started an all out war and not cared who got caught up in the crossfire.

"Why don't we kill them both?" Frost asked. Did he have to sound so enthusiastic about it? Yes, I supposed he did. That would solve some problems. Although, it would likely create others.

"That would be like playing whack-a-mole," Ramsey said. "Whatever they're up to, they're not doing it alone. If we kill them, whoever they're working with will come after us. I'm not convinced Dominic King is the head of all of this. He might think he is, but I believe someone else is pulling the strings."

"Who?" I asked. "The Fiorellis are gone, for the most part. The Bell family has more or less been absorbed into the Brantley family, thanks to the twins. No one has heard from Kurt Lasalle in years."

Kurt made a bid for power of his own, even going as far as to attack the Brantley family directly. There was more to the story, probably a lot more, but that was all I knew personally. That and somehow the attack involved Reuben's girlfriend, Mina DiMarco. I never dared ask her about it. We weren't particularly close, and I suspected she wouldn't tell me anyway. She was the ultimate closed book.

"I don't know," Ramsey said. "There's several possibilities I can think of off the top of my head. It might not even be anyone in Australia."

"But you have a suspicion," Jay said. He stood with his arms crossed, white cat fur decorating the front of his shirt.

Ramsey rubbed his chin. "The Crimson Vipers have been particularly active recently. Carlos Jones was never going to sit back and take the crumbs the Brantley family threw to him."

"The cartel." I leaned my head against Frost's shoulder. "They're the definition of unscrupulous. They deal in drugs and people. Carlos Jones would literally sell his own sister if it benefited him."

He tried to, but she ran off with her lover. I wouldn't necessarily call her my friend, but Angelina Ramirez-Jones was a woman I admired. We'd met a few times and always got along, but she was as wild as they came. She took absolutely no shit from anyone. If Mina was a closed book, Angie was a wide open one.

"It makes sense," I said finally. "Why would someone like Carlos Jones be content to be a small fish, even if it means working with people like Dominic King and Otis Skinner?"

Chances were, he'd been planning this for a long time, maybe years. Men like him lurked in the shadows, waiting and watching before they struck. His cartel wasn't called the Crimson Vipers for nothing. People on the receiving end of their bite, usually didn't live to talk about it.

"Carlos wouldn't give a shit who he's working with, as long as he got power out of it," Ramsey said. "Like you said, he'd sell his own sister. He'd sell anyone's sister. And buy them too." He pressed his lips together in disgust.

"He sounds like a hell of a guy," Frost said sarcastically. "If this asshole is behind everything, then... what does that mean?" He looked around at all of us, green eyes wide.

Sometimes, like right now, he looked much too innocent to be involved in any of this. Yeah, okay he was far from innocent, but I still wondered what his life would have been like if he hadn't gotten involved with me. Same with Storm and Dallas.

Before I came along, they were happily playing rugby and living their lives. I turned everything upside down. Introduced them to a whole new world of darkness. They deserved better than this.

If I could turn the clock back and undo all of this, would I? I'd certainly give it serious consideration.

"It means there's nothing he wouldn't do to stop us from getting in his way," I said. "I mean *nothing*. He wouldn't hesitate to kill all of us just for having this conversation if he thought he'd get away with it. At the moment, he's reliant on the Brantley family for shipments. They could stop them at any time." That would serve as a deterrent for now, but for how long?

"If he could get around them, he could do some harm," Atlas guessed.

"Exactly," I said. "No doubt they've been trying to

find a way for years. Everything that's going on now could stem from that. Dominic King might have the connections the Vipers need to provide a new route for them to receive goods."

"If we were to kill Dominic King and Otis Skinner—" Frost started.

"We'd be taking on a whole cartel," I finished for him. Now I was more scared than ever for Dallas. What the hell happened to him?

If he was dead, I'd burn this whole fucking city down, consequences be damned. He was mine. If you fuck with him, you fucked with me. My fear was gone, replaced with ice cold fury. Anger I'd carefully locked away for a long time uncoiled like a snake. When the time came to strike, I was ready. Until then, I'd wait and watch.

"What do we do now?" Frost asked.

"We find Dallas," I said.

Chapter Two

Chelsea

"Well, this shit is freaky." Storm stopped at the bottom of the stairs and looked around.

"Don't create a bottleneck," Atlas told him. He elbowed past him, through the doorway that led into my brother's workroom.

"Fuck off," Storm snapped, but it was with less heat than usual. He was too busy taking in his surroundings.

"I think this place is cool," Frost said. He grabbed Storm's hand and pulled him forward, out of the way of the rest of us.

'Cool' was one word for it, but I wasn't getting into that conversation right now. I stepped past Atlas and into the workroom.

"Hey, looks like the whole family is here," Ice

greeted cheerfully. "Sorry, most of you." He was cleaning the floor with a mop and what smelled like bleach. For once, there was no one hanging from the chains. No dead bodies lying around for us to see. No alive ones either. Just us and my brother, who appraised the men.

"You've met Frost and Storm," I said. "This is Atlas, Jay and—"

"I've met Ramsey." Ice held out his spare hand for the hooker to shake. "You're also fucking my sister?"

Ramsey shook my brother's hand and said, "Not yet."

"Be good to her," Ice told him. He looked around at the others. "That goes for all of you. Now, Dallas Gregory is missing? I put out feelers, telling people to keep an eye out for him. And to let them know anyone who does anything to him will find himself down here enjoying my company."

I stepped over to give him a hug. "Thank you. You're the best."

He squeezed me back. "I keep telling you, that's what big brothers are for. We'll find him. People tend to avoid pissing me off if possible."

"Do you really kill people down here?" Storm was still looking around. "Just like that." He snapped his fingers.

Ice grinned. "I wouldn't say it's 'just like that,' but yes. That's what generally happens in here. Which is why people try to avoid coming down here against their will. *Sometimes* it can be slightly unpleasant for them."

I snorted. "Slightly unpleasant? Only sometimes?"

"Okay, it can be very unpleasant for them all the time. But they got themselves into that situation to start with, so they generally deserve whatever happens down here." Ice leaned the mop against a side wall.

"How many?" Storm asked. When my brother raised a questioning eyebrow at him, he added, "How many people have you killed down here?"

"Three hundred and forty-two," Ice replied easily. "I keep records of all of them. I could show you if you like?" He sounded like a kid offering to show a friend his collection of marbles.

Honestly, I was pretty sure he didn't have enough marbles to call it a 'collection.' The glass kind either.

"Can we focus on Dallas for now?" I asked. "You can share your horror stories with them later. If they want to hear them."

"I do," Frost said.

Storm glanced at him but didn't say anything.

"This is all kinds of fucked up," Atlas remarked.

"Specifically, it's only thirty-two kinds of fucked up," Ice said. "I sat down once and made a list. You should have seen the look on Ares' face. He said sometimes he thinks I'm out of my mind and other times he *knows* I am. But he loves me, in his own way." Once again, he was like a child, amused at the antics of his friend.

"I'm not sure why he'd have any doubt," Storm said, half to himself.

Rather than getting offended, Ice patted him on the arm as he walked past to turn on the coffee machine in the corner of the room. "As far as I can tell, being in your right mind is overrated. Coffee anyone?"

"Ramsey was saying the Crimson Vipers have been restless recently," I said, wanting to change the subject.

"That's right," my brother agreed. "If you want to talk about people not being in their right mind, that's exactly the direction to point your fingers. I'd love to have Carlos Jones down here for the things he's done. Buying women is disgusting, even by our standards."

"Does he buy them to..." Jay grimaced, torn

between curiosity, and not wanting to know the truth.

"Whatever you can imagine him buying them for, he's doing it," Ice said.

"How does he get away with it?" Storm demanded.

"I hate to agree with Storm, but I'd like to know the same thing," Atlas said.

Both men looked at each other like they were more disgusted at being in agreement than anything Carlos Jones might do, or have done.

Ice flicked a finger back and forth between them. At the same time, he looked at me. "They don't get along?"

"That's an understatement," I said.

"They live to fight with each other," Frost said. "We've been trying to find a way to make them make peace."

"I have chains side-by-side, attached to the ceiling," Ice offered. "A couple of days hanging from them and they might find they have more in common than they realise."

"Let's call that plan F," I said.

I gave both guys the side eye so they knew I wasn't completely joking. I was just about done with them arguing. "Since they're agreeing, maybe you can answer the question."

"Ah, yes." Ice nodded. "Why does Carlos Jones get away with the things he does? Because he's useful to Reuben Brantley. Because someone has to get the drugs and other contraband out onto the streets. Otherwise Reuben might have to dirty his own hands, and God forbid he'd do that."

"There isn't someone else?" Jay asked.

"Like I said, it's whack-a-mole," Ramsey said. "Get rid of Carlos Jones and you might end up with someone worse."

"Exactly," Ice said. "Carlos is a known quantity, even if he is a repulsive excuse for a human being. If it wouldn't piss Reuben off, I'd happily end the whole cartel. That would get a little messy though. On the other hand, if Carlos Jones is behind Dominic King, then we might have a chance to be rid of him." He looked excited at the prospect. Of course he was. He might get his wish to have Carlos chained up come true.

"I'm in," Frost said. He was at least as excited as my brother.

"Me too," Atlas said quickly, as though he needed to beat Storm to it.

Storm scowled at him. "Me too," he said with a

fraction more reluctance. He wouldn't let Frost get involved unless he was and he sure as hell wouldn't let Atlas get one up on him. Nothing would get him on board faster than them speaking first.

"Where Atlas goes, I go," Jay said softly. Before I even had time to recognise the innuendo, he winked at me.

I smiled and playfully rolled my eyes at him, except now I was thinking exactly that. Both of them sliding into me...

Focus, I told myself. We needed to be concentrating on Dallas right now.

"You know I'm in," Ramsey said.

"Is there any chance the contact you sent Dallas to handed him over to the cartel?" Storm narrowed his eyes at Ramsey.

"If she did, she's dead," Ramsey said darkly. "She knows what angle I'm working. She would have to come up with some kind of story and then send him to the shelter." He nodded towards the nearby building, where the sound of dogs barking rose every few minutes.

"She?" I refused to be jealous, but I was curious.

"You might know her," Ramsey said. "India Hartman-Green. She works at Flirts, where you used to work." He said that with no hint of judgment.

Thank fuck we didn't have to have that conversation. The one where I had to admit I used to be a stripper and fucked men for money.

At this point, I'd explained myself enough times to the other guys already. My past had bothered Atlas, but the others met me there, at the club. All except Jay, who now looked at me with surprise, but not judgement either.

"I remember India," I said. "She was always happy and sweet. She loves working there." I should have guessed she worked for the Brantleys. Who else from there did? Most of them, more than likely.

"She is sweet," Ramsey agreed. "Which makes her the perfect contact. People don't like to suspect the sweet ones. One smile from her and they assume she's innocent."

"That sounds like India," I agreed. I didn't like the idea of her being drawn into anything though. Not even if she went in with her eyes open. I'd genuinely regret it if anything bad happened to her. Especially if she ended up dead. Particularly if we had to kill her for screwing over Dallas.

"You don't think Dallas would have, I don't know, become distracted with her?" Atlas asked.

"Definitely not," I said immediately.

"Not a chance," Storm agreed. "You've seen how

obsessed he is with Chelsea. He wouldn't even notice another woman, much less fuck her. He'd probably cut his own dick off first."

"Good, or I'd have to cut it off for him," my brother said. "No one gets away with cheating on my sister."

"Get in line, bro," Storm said. He pressed his meaty fists to his hips, and his lips in a tight line.

I wouldn't want to be on the receiving end of his glower.

My brother didn't blink. He cocked his head and raised an eyebrow. "I've been at the head of the line longer than you've been around, bro. But if you play nice, I'll let you help." He could have been offering to cut Storm a nice slice of cake, or offer to share finger paints with him, rather than talking about dismembering someone.

"No one needs to cut off anyone's cock," I said. "Let's go to Flirts. I want to talk to India. If Dallas went there, she might know what happened to him after that."

"I've already tried contacting her," Ramsey said. "It was the first thing I did. She's not answering either."

"Are you absolutely sure..." Atlas started. He didn't look like he wanted to finish that sentence any more than I wanted to hear the end of it. He was just throwing out possibilities to make sure we had all the positions on the field covered. Not because he really believed it was happening. That much was obvious by his expression.

"Definitely," I said. Whatever was going on here, it didn't involve Dallas and India fucking each other. "Do you have any way of knowing if he even got to Flirts?"

When Ramsey shook his head, I nodded mine. "Then that's where I'm going. Someone had to have seen him, or India. They might have some idea of what's going on."

"I'm coming with you," Frost said.

"Me too." Storm gave Atlas the side eye. "It's going to look suspicious if we all turn up at once."

"Too bad." Atlas jaw was set firm. Short of tying or chaining him up, he wasn't going to be left behind.

Jay looked equally determined. If Atlas and I were going, so was he.

Storm sighed in annoyance. "Fine, don't get in the fucking way."

"You too," Atlas said in a grunt.

Ramsey glanced at Storm, a subtle reminder of who was in charge here.

Storm rolled his eyes and didn't back down a hair.

I hoped like hell they weren't planning to start arguing with each other. The animosity between Storm and Atlas was bad enough.

"I'll keep my ears out for my contacts," Ice said. "There's a couple of people I can talk to. Keep me in the loop and I'll do the same."

"We will," I assured him. "Stay safe."

He grinned. "When have I not stayed safe? I should be saying that you, but you seem to be surrounded by some very large men with even larger muscles. I'm sure you'll be fine."

I glanced around, taking a moment to appreciate the view. "Sometimes it doesn't suck to be me." The guys were a fortress of muscle around me, protecting me. I hoped like hell I could protect them too.

I gave my brother another hug and hurried up the steps to Storm's SUV.

As I settled into a seat in the back, I couldn't shake the feeling we were being watched.

Chapter Three

Atlas

I'm not going to lie. I've been to strip clubs before. Plenty of them, but not this one. I expected Flirts to be sleazy, like so many of the others. Flashing lights, dark spaces and the stink of damp and sweat.

To my surprise, the place was almost classy. Burgundy walls, leather chairs, neatly dressed staff all in black. The smell of lavender and a hint of sex lingered in the air.

The establishment was quiet at this time of day. No one was fucking or even dancing.

Instead, the staff were carefully cleaning, washing down every surface and polishing the glasses behind the bar.

We could have been in an upscale club in any

major city in Australia.

That was fortunate, because if the place was full of customers who'd seen my woman naked, I'd have to punch them out. Don't get me started on what I'd do to any who fucked her. Suffice to say, it would hurt them, but not for long.

Yeah, I know, that was her life before me, but the idea of it still made me see red.

"This wasn't what I was expecting," Jay said out of the side of his mouth.

"Me neither," I agreed.

"It feels like we haven't been here in forever," Frost said.

I gave him the side eye. "Did you ever—" I glanced toward Chelsea.

"Not here," he said. "Only Dallas did. Storm paid, because he wanted to watch." He didn't seem to be judging his...were they boyfriends? Just stating a fact.

Storm, on the other hand, seemed very judged. He glared at Frost, as if he'd spilled state secrets, not the fullback's kink.

"What?" Frost shrugged. "That was what happened. Don't try to pretend we don't all like watching each other. I bet Atlas does, right Atlas?"

"I suppose," I agreed. So far, the only other person I saw fuck Chelsea was Jay. If I hung around with these guys for long enough, that would change. My cock stiffened at the thought. At the same time, it annoyed the crap out of me. Specifically, the idea of Storm with her made me stabby. She deserved better than him. So far, he hadn't given me any reason to change my mind about him.

"I do," Ramsey said.

Sometimes, it was easy to forget he was the only one who hadn't fucked her. He also hadn't gone out with her. Somehow, he'd slotted into our family, but I had no idea how Chelsea felt about him. Or vice versa, to be honest. That was something they'd have to figure out for themselves later.

"I thought you might." Frost shoved his shoulder into Ramsey's with familiarity, like they were old mates. Frost had a way of opening up and letting people in without stopping to think too much about it. He'd already accepted Ramsey as one of us, even if the rest of us hadn't yet.

I have to admit I liked that about him. He couldn't be more different from Storm. When he kissed me... let's just say between Chelsea, Jay and him, I was going to have a permanent erection.

"Yeah?" Ramsey raised his eyebrows at Frost.

"You know what they say about the quiet ones," Frost teased. "They're always the ones to watch."

"Truth," Jay said, his voice low, because he was one of those quiet ones.

Storm looked back at us and shook his head before turning to Chelsea. "Is she here?"

"She might be in the back," Chelsea said. She gestured toward a side door and headed in that direction.

We all hurried to keep up.

"Chelsea!" A woman with bright pink hair stepped out the door and over to give her a hug.

All five of us were immediately rigid and on guard, like the gesture flipped a switch.

Every protective instinct in my body screamed out to move closer to her. At the same time, I knew to hold back. Chelsea wouldn't have hugged the woman if she didn't know and trust her.

"Divina, you're looking well." Chelsea squeezed her, before stepping back and smiling.

"Of course I am." Divina fluffed her hair. "Haven't you heard the rumour that I drink the blood of young women so I can say beautiful?" She glanced over at me and winked.

Chelsea laughed. "That explains everything. I'll be sure to pass on your recommendation to my colleagues. Although, the legal implications might be a big hurdle to overcome."

Divina waved a hand dismissively. "This is Dusk Bay. I'd find a way if I had to. Otherwise, I'll have to start drinking the cum of young men instead." She looked us all up and down appraisingly.

"No offence, but my cum is spoken for," Frost said. He jerked his head toward Chelsea, then accompanied that with a side glance toward Storm and a small one in my direction.

Divina patted his cheek. "That's a shame. I bet you're tasty."

Frost puffed out his chest. "I am."

Chelsea shook her head at them both, no hint of jealousy in her posture or expression. I loved that she was so sure of us she wasn't bothered by some light flirting.

"Is India here?" she asked.

"Or Dallas?" Storm added.

"I don't know a Dallas, but India stepped out after we worked on her costumes this morning," Divina said. "She said something about meeting someone." She gestured with both hands, indicating she had no further information.

"She didn't tell you where she was going?" Chelsea asked.

"Not as I recall." Divina clasped her hands in front of her. "Is she in some kind of trouble?"

"We don't know yet," Chelsea said. "Probably not. It might be nothing."

"You look worried for something that's probably nothing," Divina said. "What's going on and who is Dallas?" A frown flitted over her brow. "Are you referring to Dallas Gregory? The Smashers player?"

"That's him," I said. "We're trying to find him. India might be able to help." Had I said too much? I didn't know if we could trust this woman or not.

Chelsea answered that question when she said, "Yes, we are. He was supposed to meet us and he didn't show. We're worried."

"I see," Divina said slowly. "If India is involved in something she shouldn't be, I'm going to—"

Her words were interrupted by a high pitched scream.

My high alert doubled. I stepped closer to Chelsea, shielding her with my body as the others did the same. I didn't care that I was almost pressed against Storm, as long as she was safe.

"That can't be good," Frost said.

I grunted in agreement. "Where did that come from?"

Divina raised a shaky finger and pointed at the door she'd appeared through. "There."

"I'll look," Ramsey said quickly.

He didn't seem scared. If anything, he seemed curious, but cautious at the same time. Only his body language indicated any concern, but that was for Chelsea's safety. He stood between her and the door, another protective shield.

"Not by yourself," Storm insisted. "If you go, we all go."

Ramsey gave him half a glance before nodding and heading over to place his hand on the doorknob. He paused, listening carefully before turning it and pushing. The door opened easily, and no other screams sounded from that part of the club.

Yet.

He stepped in first, the rest of us crowding around, everyone trying to fit through the door at the same time. Everyone except Jay, who hung back to avoid the press of bodies. I followed his cue, staying back and letting the others pass before we went through ourselves.

The back of the club was nothing special. An open doorway showed shelves covered in dozens of boxes. Some open, others not. Several were full of unused glassware. They sat pressed hard against boxes full of condoms.

That brought me back to Chelsea, and other men

fucking her, but I shoved the thought away. I didn't need the rage right now.

Focus, I told myself.

"That leads to the cellar." Chelsea was pointing toward another door. "There's another that leads backstage." Her face was paler than usual.

I grabbed her arm. "You don't have to go in there. Whatever happened, we can deal with it."

"I'm okay," she said a bit too quickly. "They might need a doctor."

I wanted to argue with her and keep her back from whatever happened, but she was right. Her skills might be needed now.

For a moment, I wished she was anything but a doctor. Okay, except a stripper. Couldn't she have become a dog walker, or work in an ice cream shop? Anything that would give me an excuse to throw her over my shoulder and take her out of here.

"Stay close to me," I told her.

"And me," Storm added. For once, he wasn't scowling at me. His attention was on the door up ahead, body tense.

I knew that posture; I saw it on the field so many times. He was ready to act, to deal with whatever was thrown at us.

I didn't like him, but I respected him. He wouldn't run from potential danger.

With Chelsea and Divina between us, Frost and Jay behind, and Ramsey in the lead, we moved toward the other door, footsteps careful, senses open.

Ramsey put a hand on the door handle and turned to nod to us to be ready.

I nodded back and held my breath as he pushed the door inwards.

We were met with silence. No sound, no motion. No screaming, no one jumping out at us. Nothing.

That in itself put me on edge. Whatever I was expecting, it wasn't *nothing*.

Ramsey peered around before stepping through the doorway and waving for us to follow.

I took Chelsea's hand and tucked her in closer to me as we stepped across the threshold, into the backstage area.

"Hello?" Ramsey called out.

The word was met with silence.

"They might be in the dressing room," Divina whispered.

Chelsea glanced at her and nodded. "It's just down there." She pointed a few metres ahead.

"Can I convince you to stay here?" I asked. It seemed unlikely, but I had to try. If only because I was ninety-nine percent certain Storm was about to. I wasn't going to let him get in first. Not to mention, whatever was down there might be something she shouldn't go near.

"Nope," she said before anyone else could speak. She squeezed my hand and pulled me along behind Ramsey.

Moving more quickly now, we stepped down the corridor and into the small dressing room. Racks of costumes lined the walls on either side. Two tables were pressed apart against a mirror, chairs at each. Lights hung over the tables to help people see when they put on their make-up. At least, that's what I was guessing they were for. It was definitely not my area of expertise.

A small window looked out over the street behind the club. It was open, letting in a brisk breeze, rippling curtains which hung to either side.

"I can't see any—" I started.

Chelsea let out a squeak and let go of my hand. She hurried over to a small bathroom to the side of the dressing room.

I made a grab for her, but she moved too quickly, leaving me no choice but to trot a few steps to follow.

"Don't need a doctor," Ramsey remarked. He looked down at the floor and shook his head.

No one could refute his observation. Once a person was dead, chest sliced open down the heart, there was nothing any doctor could do. Not even a really good one.

"It's..." Frost grimaced.

"Fuck," Chelsea whispered. She put a hand over her mouth and shook her head. Her eyes shone with tears. "It was."

Chapter Four

Chelsea

India's blonde hair fanned out around her head. Her eyes were open, staring. Her clothes, a simple white T-shirt and a pair of track pants, were quickly soaking up the blood that pooled on the floor around her.

I was still staring in horror, and the same anger I felt at the park, when I became aware of the guys stepping around me, moving carefully.

"Whoever did this might be close," Ramsey said.

His words took a few moments to seep into my brain.

Of course, India was the one who screamed. Right before she was—

I swallowed hard. My stomach felt like it was in a knot. I saw dead people before, and badly injured ones, but nothing like this. Not someone I considered a friend. The last time I saw her, she was so full of life and excitement, and now, all of that was gone.

"If Dallas is..." Frost shook his head.

"He's not," Storm insisted. "He's *not* fucking dead."

I blinked. Tears trickled down my cheeks. Grief and fury, barely balanced by Storm's assurance. I didn't want to think Dallas was dead either, but if India was dead and he was still missing, it was all too painfully possible.

"He'll turn up," Atlas said softly, his mouth near my ear. "Tex is tougher than that."

"So was India," I said. "And... Sadie." I looked over to Divina, my eyes wide.

"It's her day off," Divina said. "She said something about visiting family in Melbourne."

I nodded. When we stepped out of here, I'd call her and make sure she was okay. Maybe tell her to stay away for a little while. Until all of this blew over. How long would that be? That was anyone's guess. It could be days.

It might be never.

"Is there anywhere here someone could hide?" Storm asked. "Or another way out?"

"There's a door that leads out to the loading bay," Divina said. She nodded in that direction.

"Storm and I will go and look," Ramsey said. "Frost, Atlas, Jay: stay with Chelsea."

I wanted to tell them to stay with me too, but I couldn't. Whoever did this to India might still be close. This might be our only chance to catch them. When we did...

"Be careful," was all I could say.

"Always." Storm kissed my mouth and gave me a tight squeeze.

To my surprise, Ramsey did the same, planting a lingering kiss to my lips. "Won't be long." He gestured to Storm before they both stepped out of the bathroom and back to the corridor.

It was Frost who wrapped his arms around me and pulled me to him. "I'm so sorry this happened to your friend."

I closed my eyes and rested my head on his shoulder. "I'm sorry too. This whole thing, it's fucked up." That was the understatement of the year. Was it too late to grab all of my guys and get the hell out of Dusk Bay? I didn't care where we went, as long as it was away from here. To hell with burning the place down. We'd only get singed if we tried. Choked on the smoke.

"We'll find them," he assured me. "And when we do, they'll end up worse than her. I'll see to it personally."

"Don't do anything stupid," I said. "I don't want any of you getting hurt or killed. There's been enough death already." The smell of India's blood started to turn my stomach.

"I have no intention of getting hurt," he said. "I'm pretty sure I can say the same for the others. I know Storm would be pissed off if anyone tried to kill him."

"So would I," Atlas said.

"You'd be pissed off if someone tried to kill Storm?" Jay asked.

Atlas snorted. "That wasn't what I meant, but sure. I'd be pissed off if someone tried to kill any of us. We might be a fucked up family, but we're a family. If anyone messes with one of us, they mess with all of us. Even Storm."

"I knew you'd end up friends," Frost said. After a moment, he added, "Or maybe more."

"Not more," Atlas said, sounding definite. "We'll learn to tolerate each other for Chelsea's sake. That's all."

"I hope you learn to like each other for your own sakes," I said.

The fighting was starting to get on my nerves.

Friendly rivalry was one thing, nipping at each other like a pair of dogs was another. Maybe I should threaten to have them neutered. They might try harder to be nice to each other then.

"There's no sign of anyone out there," Storm said, as he and Ramsey re-entered the dressing room. "If they went out that way, they're gone."

I sighed softly, inhaling Frost's scent, a hint of sweat and a lot of masculinity. "We may never know who killed her. Or where Dallas is."

"The back of the club has cameras?" Jay asked.

"Of course," Divina said. "I'll have my security check the footage." She pulled out her phone and sent off a text.

"Have it forwarded to me," Ramsey said. "I'll have a look at it. If we can get a good image from that, we might find whoever they were."

Divina nodded and tapped her screen again before putting her phone back in her skirt pocket. "They'll send everything they find from the last couple of hours. It might show your friend Dallas."

"Good thinking," Frost told her.

She smiled, but it didn't reach her eyes. "Thanks." His smile faded completely when she glanced down toward India's body. "She was one of my best girls. First Ivy, now India."

Frost shifted uncomfortably in my arms at the mention of Ivy.

"I don't suppose I can convince you to come back for a while?" Divina asked me.

"No," Storm and Atlas said at the same time.

"Not a fucking chance," Storm growled. "She's with us now. We don't want her taking her clothes off for other men." He turned his best scowl on her.

She returned it with a flat stare. "I don't remember asking you. My question was directed to Chelsea, who's more than capable of making up her own mind. A fact you should be well aware of if you know her at all."

Storm gaped at her, his face turning pink. He looked as though he was about to verbally tear her a new one.

"I'm not coming back," I said quickly, trying to diffuse the situation. "I'm done with stripping. But I'll help out any other way, if I can. Even if it's only a shoulder for people to cry on." That seemed to appease Storm, for now.

Divina gave Storm a long, last look before turning and heading out the door. "I'll need to organise someone to handle India's remains." She swept away without another glance.

"What do we do now?" Frost asked.

"I have to speak to Otis Skinner," Ramsey said. "If he hears about this from someone else first, he'll wonder why. He'll see this as an attack on his plans." He seemed particularly unimpressed.

"Is that what this is?" I asked. "Someone thought she was working for him and went after her?"

"Or someone knew she was working with me." He looked down regretfully.

"They might come after you next," I said softly. This was getting worse by the minute.

"What I can't figure out is what Dallas has to do with any of this," Frost said.

"If he was seen talking to India, they may have made assumptions," I said. He might really be dead after all.

Frost brushed hair off the side of my face. "He's okay. He'll turn up soon, I promise."

"You might not be able to keep that promise," I pointed out.

I wanted him to, I wanted it badly. If Dallas was right in front of me now, I'd grab hold of him and never let go. Would it be strange if I handcuffed myself to him for the rest of our lives?

Probably, but I'd be tempted to do it anyway, so he'd never be out of my sight again. I'd consider letting him out to train and play, but only for a few hours at a time. I had a feeling he wouldn't mind being attached to me like that.

Okay, I wouldn't do that, but I still wished he was here with us.

"I never make promises I can't keep," he said. "There's a logical explanation for him disappearing. He could be at home right now, having a nap. Or he might be looking at that mansion we were talking about, and putting in an offer. We might be the proud owners of a big, fancy house on the cliff as we speak." He seemed to like the idea.

"Why didn't he turn up at the animal shelter then?" Jay reasoned.

"He slept through it, then went to buy the mansion," Frost said. "He was already late, so figured why bother? Buying property is much more fun, especially when he gets to give Chelsea the keys as a surprise."

It was a stretch, and we all knew it, but none of us had the heart to say so. Not when we all hoped it was the truth, or somewhere close to it.

"Do you want someone to go with you?" I asked Ramsey. "I don't like the idea of any of us being alone right now."

We wouldn't be very subtle if we moved around Dusk Bay in a group, but it would be more difficult for anyone to try to attack us. Especially if they were one person, acting alone. They'd either be very brave or very stupid to take on five big football players and a tall doctor.

Stupid, or desperate.

Ramsey took my hand and pulled me gently from Frost's arms. He wrapped his around me and pressed his mouth to mine. "I'll be fine. When I'm done with Otis Skinner, I'm going to claim you." He kissed me again, his tongue tasting my lips before he let me go and stepped back.

"Keep her safe," he told the others.

"Always," Atlas assured him. "Keep yourself safe."

"Always," Ramsey echoed. He stepped through the dressing room again and out the doorway. His footsteps sounded on the concrete floor before he pushed out the loading bay door and let it close behind him with a clang.

I tried to tell myself there was nothing final about that clang. We'd see him again in a couple of hours, safe and well. Ready to claim me and own me, like the other guys had already.

"Let's go home," Storm said. "If Dallas is there having a nap, I'm going to punch him in the cock."

"After you tell him how glad you are to see him," I said.

He grunted. "Maybe."

"I'll be glad to see him," Frost said. "But I might let Storm punch him in the cock after all this worry."

"No one is punching anyone in the cock," I said. "Not unless they're on the other side. Then you can do all the cock punching and kicking you like."

Frost pumped the air with his fist. "Hell yeah. Let's do it." He was clearly looking forward to raising some hell and getting his hands dirty.

"I need to be out of here," Jay said. He walked ahead of us, scanning the area as he went. Even stopping to push at the racks of costumes before walking past. "Just checking to see if anyone is hiding in there." If they were, they would have gotten a fist to the kidneys, or to the face if they were crouched down amongst the fabric.

Since no one cried out in pain, I presumed no one was there. Most of the costumes were too skimpy to hide behind anyway.

I took a moment to glance back at India and mouth her a silent apology. Was there anything I could have done to prevent her death? Was there anything anyone could have done?

Maybe if Ramsey hadn't sent Dallas to her, she would have gone unnoticed. Or would she?

This might not have anything to do with Dominic King or Carlos Jones. It might be a jealous former boyfriend or customer who killed her. Or a random attack on an innocent woman. I didn't like any of those options either, and I sensed this wasn't random or anything to do with jealousy. Her death had something to do with us. What, I didn't know.

I wish we'd come here sooner. A couple of minutes earlier and we might have stopped her killer before they took her life. She might be alive right now. They might be dead instead. Or on their way to my brother's workroom. Or—

Fuck only knew how many possible scenarios we could have prevented, or brought to fruition. In the end, we weren't here in time and India paid the price.

How many other people were going to die before this was done?

And where the hell was Dallas?

Chapter Five

Chelsea

"I'll tell you where he *isn't*." Frost appeared from the room Dallas claimed as his own, green eyes full of regret and disappointment. He held onto his hope Dallas was there for the entire drive home. Now that hope was dashed, he looked like a lost boy who misplaced his puppy.

I had to remind myself he'd killed a woman. Daniel Frost was no lost, innocent boy.

"He isn't in any of the bedrooms." Frost rubbed a hand over the back of his neck, frowning as though sure he missed something.

"Neither of the bathrooms either." I sighed. I hadn't expected to find him there, but I checked anyway. Grateful at least not to find him in the bath, under the water, or lying dead in the shower.

"His car isn't parked in his space." Storm dropped his keys on the kitchen island, where they clattered across the granite surface.

For the hundredth time, I checked my phone. No notifications. No text messages, no missed calls. Nothing from Dallas, Ramsey or my brother.

Nothing.

I flopped down on the couch and cradled my face in my hands. Not losing my shit was taking everything I had. Usually, I was good at remaining calm in a crisis. My job relied on it. This? This was getting to me more and more. Unravelling me slowly.

The longer we went without answers, the more difficult it became to keep my composure. The more I wanted to tip my head back and scream in frustration. I wanted to walk the streets of Dusk Bay until I'd been everywhere he could possibly be and even places he couldn't. I wanted to get everyone in the city out to look for him. And to look for whoever killed India.

I was good at a lot of things, but dealing with the feeling of helplessness was not one of them. I hated that I couldn't fix any of this.

"I'll try calling him again," Frost said. He sat down on the coffee table in front of me and held his device to his ear. He frowned slightly as he listened to it ring. Shook his head as it went to voicemail. He opened his mouth, as though considering leaving a message, but closed it again and ended the call.

We left enough messages on Dallas' voicemail already. One more wouldn't make him answer them sooner.

I sighed heavily. All I wanted right now was for him to walk through the door and tell me he was fine. That he got distracted and lost track of time. A long walk on the beach. A training session at the gym. Something.

Anything.

Jay sat down beside me, close enough for comfort, but giving me space at the same time. "I don't know Tex all that well, but I'm sure he'll be fine."

"What Jay said." Atlas sat on the other side of me, his thigh touching mine. "We're Smashers, we don't give up without a fight. We're tough as old boots. Better looking though."

Frost stared at him.

Atlas stared back. "What? You've never heard anyone compare themselves to old boots before?"

"That's the first time I've heard you call yourself a Smasher," Frost said. "That you've admitted you're one of us."

Atlas shrugged. "It's the first time I've felt like one of us. Part of the team."

"Me too," Jay said softly. "Part of the family." He glanced up at Storm, as if expecting him to contradict them.

Storm didn't. If he wasn't happy about it, he was resigned. We were a family, whether he liked it or not.

"One big happy family," Frost said, with a hint of irony.

Big, yes. Happy... Not right now. Not when we were separated and still somewhat divided.

"I'm going to go down and see if Dallas is in the gym, or the pool," Storm said.

I jerked my face towards him. "You shouldn't go alone." I didn't want him to go missing too.

"I'll be fine," he said. "I'm not leaving the building."

"Chelsea is right," Frost said. "None of us should do anything alone. I'll go with you." He placed his hands on his thighs, ready to stand.

"No, I'll go," Atlas said. "Like you said, we're a family. It's time for Storm and I to try to get along."

"Okay." Frost lowered his arms. "No killing each other down there."

"I won't if he won't." Storm gave Atlas the side

eye, but waited for him to reach the front door before opening it and stepping out.

"I won't if Storm isn't a dickhead," Atlas said before the door closed behind them.

"What are the chances Storm can avoid being a dickhead for ten minutes?" Jay asked.

"He's okay when you get to know him," Frost told him. "The question is, what are we going to do for the next ten minutes? I vote you and I take Chelsea's mind off all of this for a little while."

"I vote for that too." Jay's eyes darkened, but his expression was tentative. Not when he looked at me, but his sidelong glance at Frost. The way his tongue swiped over his lower lip.

"I'd never ask you to do anything you're not comfortable with," Frost told him. "Let's make this about Chelsea."

"Deal." Judging by the expression on Jay's face, that was the end of the conversation, but only for now. They'd work that out when they were ready. For now, Jay let his hand wander up my thigh and under the hem of my shirt.

Frost placed his hands on my knees and slowly moved them up, pushing the fabric with him as he went.

We should have focused on Dallas and how to

find him, but the moment their hands touched my skin, my whole body was on fire.

Everyone was doing what they could to find him. I'd allow myself a few minutes to feel good with two of my guys.

"She's so wet," Frost said to Jay as he revealed the gusset of my panties. He pressed the tip of his finger under the lace and over the entrance to my pussy.

"Her pussy is beautiful," Jay whispered reverently. "So perfect. And that piercing is something else." When Frost pushed my panties aside, Jay leaned down to my clit piercing, before drawing it between his lips and sucking gently.

That was almost enough to make me come on the spot. My back arched and I moaned. "Holy shit, that's..." I had no further words. All coherent thoughts were pushed right out of my mind. The only thing left was to feel.

"I think she likes it," Frost said.

"Good." Jay circled my piercing with the tip of his tongue, before sucking again.

I was already quivering, but that increased twofold when Frost pulled down the front of my blouse and bra, and started to lavish attention on my nipples.

"You're right, she is wet," Jay said as he slipped a

finger inside me, then another. "Is she always this wet?"

"Basically permanently," Frost agreed. "She's always ready for us. Always willing."

"I knew she was perfect." Jay sat back and watched himself fuck me with his fingers.

After a moment, Frost did the same, both avidly watching them slide in and out of me.

"That's so hot," Frost said. "She's taking those so well. She always does."

"She's taking them very well," Jay agreed. He added a third finger, thrusting slightly slower.

"Can I see how well she takes your cock?" Frost asked.

Jay's eyes widened, but he slowly slid his fingers out of me and pushed down the front of his track pants and briefs. He grabbed my hips and pulled me to the edge of the couch before sliding me onto his cock. He positioned us carefully so I was lying back and he and Frost could watch his cock slide in and out of me.

"Even better than I imagined," Frost whispered. "I could watch her being fucked all day."

"I could fuck her all day," Jay said. "Why don't you...rub her clit and make her come for us?"

Frost scooted around a little so he could slide his

hand between my legs and rub the pad of his thumb over my clit without taking his eyes off Jay's thrusts.

"Yes, just like that," Jay said, his voice strained.

"You heard the man," Frost said. He kept up his motion on my clit while leaning over to suck one of my nipples.

I couldn't have stopped myself and I didn't want to. My whole body clenched, muscles tight around Jay's cock as I came hard. I rocked my hips as carefully as I could, knowing they were both watching me, and watching Jay's cock as he exploded inside me.

He moaned. "Fuck... So good... So fucking good." He ground against me, drawing out both of our orgasms for as long as he could. He came down slowly and carefully, breathing as evenly as he could while still keeping his gaze on where we were connected.

"Can I see?" Frost asked. He took his hand off my clit and rested it lightly on my thigh. "I want to see your cum inside her pussy."

Jay pulled back slowly, while keeping my knees apart so they could both watch as his cum slowly trickled back out of me.

"Now that is beautiful," Frost marvelled. "She deserves to be decorated with cum." He pushed his pants down and pulled out his cock. He wrapped his fist around it and gave a few short tugs, sliding his hand up and down his length. With a grunt, he came, adding his release to Jay's. Letting their cum mingle on the outside of my pussy.

"Work of art," Jay said approvingly. His eyes were dark and his cock was already starting to harden again.

"I thought so," Frost said with a smile. "We can both fill her next time. So full until she overflows."

"You guys are too good to me," I whispered.

"You're amazing," Frost told me. "You deserve to be fucked all day and all night. And then some."

"So do you," I said to them both. I wanted them to fuck me until I couldn't walk for a week. And neither could they.

"We should get you cleaned up," Frost said with a regretful sigh. "The other guys should be back soon."

As they helped me up off the couch and to the bathroom to wash my pussy clean, reality slowly crept back into my brain.

Had Storm and Atlas found Dallas yet? I already felt as though they'd been gone for too long. What if something happened to them while we were fucking?

Chapter Six

Atlas

The whole way down, Storm and I stayed on opposite sides of the elevator. He stood with his arms crossed, head tilted back, eyes toward the ceiling.

I leaned against the wall, hands by my sides, looking half at him, half at the panel beside him. Slowly, the numbers counted down to the ground floor, then the gym below that.

The elevator pinged cheerfully before the doors slid open.

We exchanged glances, both waiting for the other to get out first.

When the doors started to close again, I reached out to stop them. Hand between them, I gestured for him to step out in front of me.

He looked like he might object, but finally

pushed past me and out of the carriage. "Gym's that way." He jerked his head to the left.

"No shit," I said. Right in front of us was a large sign that pointed the way. To the right was the indoor pool for the apartment building.

He glared at me for a moment before shrugging and stomping off to the left.

"Are you going to get your head out of your ass at some point?" I said to his back.

"My head isn't in my ass," he said without slowing.

"Could have fooled me," I muttered.

"Wouldn't be hard," he muttered back.

"What is your fucking problem?" I growled.

He stopped so suddenly I almost ran into him. He turned around slowly and glared at me. "My problem is that you've had an attitude since you joined the team. Every chance you get to take a dig, you take it."

"You too," I pointed out. "You never wanted Jay and I on the team in the first place."

"I didn't give a shit." He dropped his hands to his sides. "I wanted good players who wanted to be Smashers. Because I give a shit about the team. Always have. It was the first fucking thing I thought about when I woke up and the last fucking thing I thought about when I went to bed. Then you and Jay rocked up with chips on your shoulders the size of Tasmania, like you were too good for us. Like all you fucking wanted was to go back to Sydney and be a Devil again."

"You know why we transferred," I said.

"Yeah, I do. You admitted that even with a mission to do, you didn't want to be here." His gaze bore into me.

"Now that's changed." I glared back at him. "I want to be here. I want to be a part of the team and this family. I want to be with Chelsea."

"Maybe it's too little too late for that," he said.

"I don't believe in 'too late'," I said. "Maybe we didn't have the best attitude when we arrived in Dusk Bay—"

"No 'maybe' about it," he snapped. "You had shitty attitudes. You made it a them versus us thing. You stalked around like a caged animal. As if you couldn't walk away if you wanted to."

"I couldn't," I argued. "I had commitments and a contract. Same as you do. You couldn't have walked away either."

"I didn't want to walk away," he snarled. "If I was on a different team this season, I'd give them everything. Because that's what I fucking do. I put everything I have into...everything. Footy, Chelsea, all of this mobster shit. If I'm in, I'm all the way in."

"Not everyone can be like you," I pointed out. "Not all of us are single-minded." Some of us had other priorities, whether we liked it or not.

"It's not hard to make a commitment." His own tone evened out slightly. "You just make it and stick to it. That's all. It's not rocket science."

"I have made a commitment," I said. "I'm committed to the same things you are. I'm all in too. How do you think Chelsea feels being stuck between us? Having to mediate our bullshit? Or Frost? He doesn't like it either. I've seen it on his face." And a lot of other things, including lust. "It upsets Jay too."

Storm exhaled long and slow. He placed his palm on the wall beside him and braced himself. "You think I'm just going to, what? Be your best friend from now on?"

"Why not?" I said jokingly. "I'm pretty fucking awesome."

I deserved the snort he gave in response to my sarcasm. "Can we try to be civil to each other? That doesn't seem like too much to ask, for the good of everyone."

His brow crinkled and he looked down at the worn carpet on the floor. "I'll think about it."

"That's all I ask," I said. Okay, I wanted him to try, not just *think* about it, but it was a start.

He looked up at me. "You have to stop being a smartass. If you're one of us, you need to act like it. We were lucky the first couple of games, but if we don't start playing like a real team, we're going to get smashed. On and off the field."

He didn't need to explain what he meant. If we didn't have each other's backs, we'd end up like India. I wished I could have spared Chelsea from having to see her friend like that. Doctor or no doctor, she was still disturbed by it. Still heartbroken. I knew she blamed herself, even though none of it was her fault. There was nothing she or any of us could have done. We got there too late. Next time, we'd be quicker.

"Yeah," I said.

I hated to admit it, but he was right. He'd been a dickhead, but so had I. I had exactly the chip on my shoulder he'd accused me of having. And then some, if I was honest. I was ripped out of a place I loved and thrown here. I resented the Smashers, and the Brantley family. It was easier to hide in a corner with Jay and pretend we were better than everyone else. I'd even harboured a fantasy that we dealt with Dominic King and anyone working with him, before going back to the Sydney Devils.

Now I knew that was a stupid fantasy. My life was here, in Dusk Bay with my team, my woman and Jay. Frost as well. I couldn't imagine going back to Sydney. I wouldn't go back. If they tried to send me, I'd have more than a chip on my shoulder.

"We should keep looking for Tex." Storm shoved himself off the wall and started off towards the gym.

I followed, keeping an eye on the direction we'd come. It would suck if an attacker came up behind us while we were focused on what was ahead. Nothing we couldn't handle, of course, but it would be a distraction we didn't need.

Storm pulled a card out of his pocket and waved it in front of the lock on the door to open it. A light flashed green and the lock clicked before Storm pushed the door open and leaned his upper body inside.

After a moment, he stepped the rest of the way in, holding the door so I could do the same.

The gym was amazing. All of the equipment was state-of-the-art and well-maintained. A couple of treadmills stood on one side of the room and several stationary bikes on the other. A rack full of weights took up space in the back corner, beside a basket of yoga mats. Along one wall was a large screen TV, with the sound on, the screen running an infomercial for a food slicer. Apparently if I bought now, I'd get a free set of steak knives. I made a note to check out the slicer later, it looked useful.

The room was empty.

"There's a bathroom in the back," Storm said.

We exchanged glances. I suspected we both had the same thought. We wouldn't find Dallas in there, but we might as well look.

This time, I led the way across the gym and through the door to the bathroom at the back of the space.

"Dallas?" I called out.

No answer. I hadn't expected one. The place was too quiet for anyone to be in here and alive.

I turned and shook my head. "He's not here either."

"Let's try the pool." Storm headed back across the gym with me at his heels. We stepped out the door, careful to close it behind us, and started back down the corridor and past the elevator.

"This building has nice facilities," I remarked.

"The best," he agreed. "That's why I live here. That and the view."

"Can't beat that." I noticed the view when I was in his apartment a few minutes ago. "I'm starting to think Dusk Bay might be nicer than Sydney."

He snorted. "Of course it fucking is. I'd rather be here than anywhere else." He stopped in front of a pair of wide glass doors that looked straight into the pool area.

"I might have to buy myself an apartment here." I pressed my face so close to the glass, it fogged up. I pulled back, wiped it clear, and peered again. "It doesn't look like there's anyone in there."

"Just in case." Storm pulled out his card and unlocked this door before pushing it open and stepping into the steamy space.

The smell of chlorinated water hit like a wave that made me wrinkle my nose. I preferred an outdoor pool without chlorine, but this would be perfect in winter. Fortunately, my hair was dark enough that it didn't turn green after swimming. Not like my sisters' hair. I briefly wondered if Frost's hair turned green in chlorine too.

"There's no one floating in there," I said gratefully. No football player face down and lifeless. No innocent women either. I wouldn't have minded finding Dominic King floating here, but I wasn't that lucky today. Give it time, he might end up that way at some point.

"Not today," Storm agreed. "An apartment two floors down from mine is for sale." He said it with reluctance, but the fact he volunteered the information at all was a minor miracle.

We both knew I could have done a search on my phone and found it, so for him to mention it was a big deal. One I decided not to call too much attention to, other than an appreciative dip of my head.

"I'll look into it. This is a great place to work out." I stepped closer to the pool, peering into the clear blue water. It lapped softly against the side of the pool, almost hypnotic. I would have loved nothing more than to strip down to my underwear and dive in for a few laps.

"Don't fall in." He'd find it hilarious if I did.

I glanced over at him and rolled my eyes, but for once there was no animosity in it. This was almost friendly banter between teammates. Something we'd never achieved before. That was progress. I'd mark it on my calendar if I had one.

"I'm guessing there's a change room here." In a building like this, they wouldn't want residents walking around, dripping pool water on the carpet.

"Yep." Storm waved toward matching doors on the side of the pool area. "I'll check the men's change room." He almost seemed to be issuing a challenge.

"I have no problem checking the women's." I

grinned. The way our voices echoed, we were the only ones in here anyway.

"Not surprised." He smirked like he won somehow and headed into the male change room.

I tapped on the door before pushing it open and stepping into the other.

"Shit."

Chapter Seven

Chelsea

Frost grabbed my hand before I skidded on the pool deck. He didn't tell me to slow down, or make a joke about running beside the pool. Instead, he kept me upright and trotted with me into the change area.

My heart in my throat, I pushed the door open.

Atlas and Storm crouched beside Dallas, who sat slumped on the floor in the corner. His face was covered in blood, his hazel eyes staring without seeing.

"Is he—" Frost started.

"He's alive," Storm said. "I'm not a doctor, but I think he's in shock."

I stepped over carefully and knelt down in front of him. "Dallas? Are you okay?"

Slowly, slowly he lifted his head and looked at me. At first, his eyes were vacant. Gradually, recognition dawned.

He launched himself at me, wrapping his arms around my neck. His whole body shook.

I clung on to him, trying to keep from being pushed over backwards. He was heavy and his grip was desperate. I hung on until his trembling started to abate. Keeping him close and occasionally whispering soft, soothing words.

"Chelsea," he groaned.

"I'm right here." I ran a hand up and down his back. "It's okay. Are you all right? What happened?"

"Chelsea," he said again. "She came at me."

"Who came at you?" I asked gently.

I could have been talking to a child who accidentally did something wrong and was terrified of being punished for it. I reminded myself he was anything but a child. Whatever happened, we'd deal with it.

He leaned back just enough to look me in the eyes. Close enough our noses were almost touching.

"Ramsey told me to talk to India," he whispered. "To pretend I was working with him and Otis Skinner." He frowned. "I don't think he's working with Otis Skinner." He seemed confused.

"He's not," I said, as reassuring as I could. "You made it to Flirts then?"

"Yeah." His expression and tone were vague, like he couldn't quite recall if he had or not. "I did. I was supposed to go to the animal shelter." He looked slightly frantic now, like he realised he was running late and was about to get up and bolt for the door.

"It's okay, we took care of it," I said quickly. "The PR is done."

"Oh." He relaxed a fraction. "I'm sorry, I should have been there."

"Why weren't you?" Atlas asked. "What did India say?"

Dallas tipped his head back to look up at him.

"She agreed to tell Otis I was there, and that Ramsey gave us both a job to do," Dallas said slowly. "Then—" He shook his head, brushing the tip of his nose over mine.

"Then what?" I gripped his back and held him carefully, silently telling him I'd support him no matter what he had to say.

"She thought I left," he said. "But there was something about her. It seemed... Off. I was going to leave, but I stayed to listen. She was talking to someone else."

"Who?" Atlas asked.

Dallas' frown deepened. "I don't know, I couldn't hear. She told them about me and said she was going to tell Otis Skinner everything I said to her. She was going to confirm his suspicions that Ramsey isn't working with him."

"She was working with Skinner," I concluded softly. I didn't want to believe it, but I trusted Dallas. If that was what he overheard, then it was true.

"I thought maybe she was saying those things to put Skinner off," Dallas said. "She was supposed to be pretending to work with him. I—" He swallowed hard. "I went back in to talk to her. She was still on the phone. She ended the call." His eyes were glazed again as he thought back, trying to get his thoughts and memories straight.

"I confronted her. Asked her whose side she was on. She laughed it off and said she was on the same side as me. But then I told her I was working with Otis Skinner and Dominic King. She seemed surprised, but she said she was too. They paid her well to stay loyal. She said she was going to get out of stripping because they paid her so much money. Then she asked about someone I've never heard of. It was a test. If I was really working for them, I'd know.

I tried to pretend, but she saw right through me. Then she grabbed up a knife and she came at me."

He closed his eyes. "She took me by surprise, but I overpowered her. I got the knife from her and then... I don't know what happened next. One minute she was staring at the knife in my hand, and the next she screamed. She lunged for the knife. Then she was dead."

"Fuck," Storm whispered.

"Yeah," Frost agreed. He put a hand on Dallas' bicep. "It happens so quickly, you don't even know it's happening until it's done. And then you wonder... What the fuck do I do next?"

Dallas opened red rimmed eyes and looked over at him. "Yeah. I panicked. I ran. Threw the knife in the first rubbish bin I found, and ran. I didn't know where I was going, but I ended up here."

"I'm glad you did," I said. "We were worried about you. You didn't answer your phone."

He blinked a couple of times, confused again. "I don't know where it is. I lost it... Somewhere. I don't remember if I had it after I ran. Everything is blank."

"Don't push yourself," I said. "It'll come back to you. We should find that knife though. In case the police find it first."

"I'll tell Ice," Frost said. "He'll know how to deal with it."

"We need to let Ramsey know," Atlas said. "He went to see Otis Skinner. He might be walking into something. Whoever India was talking to, might have gone to him when she didn't."

"I'll call him," Storm said. He rose to his feet and took a few steps away.

"Do you remember the name of the person India asked you about?" I asked Dallas. "They could be important."

He thought for a moment. "I think it was... Nile Fox?"

I pressed my lips together, trying to figure out why that name rang a vague bell. Whatever it was, it didn't come to me. Nothing more than that I heard it before. Ramsey or my brother might have a better idea who they were.

"Ramsey is on his way back," Storm said. "It seems Otis Skinner is pissed off because someone killed his minion."

Dallas flinched.

"She would have killed you," I said. "She came at you with a knife, you did what you had to do." He was a big guy, he might have overpowered her, but if she was desperate, who knows what she might have done. She could have had another knife, or a gun. She could have waited until he turned his back before using it.

When it came down to it, did it matter? She was dead and he wasn't. If she was working for Dominic King and Otis Skinner, then she would have ended up dead sooner or later anyway. If not by us, then by someone else.

"I'm not sure," he said. "I tried talking to her, but she wouldn't listen. I could have called for help. Or tied her up, or... something."

"Either way, she'd still be dead," I said. "If you hesitated and hadn't bolted, they might have seen you. There's a greater chance they would have known who killed her. They'd be hunting for you as we speak. Right now, they have no idea it was you."

"I suppose." He put his hand on the back of my head and pulled me in closer, until our noses were touching again, and his breath was on my mouth. "I should hate myself for killing her. But I don't."

"You shouldn't hate yourself," I assured him. "You survived. That was all you could do."

"Dallas?" Frost crept in closer. "Did you enjoy it? Is that what got you freaked out?"

Dallas huffed out a warm breath that tickled my cheek. "I didn't want to."

"Neither did I when I killed Ivy," Frost said. "But I did. Honestly, I'm a bit jealous of you. I bet Atlas is too. He didn't seem to hate killing Bruce Fergus."

In the corner of my eye, Atlas shifted uncomfortably. "I prefer not to kill women." He huffed out a breath. "Chelsea is right, you did what you had to do. To protect yourself and all of us. If she spoke to Otis Skinner, we'd all be fucked right now. We're not, because of you."

He took a couple of steps closer and crouched down. "I can tell you, killing for the first time, that's the hardest one. It gets easier after that. Eventually, you stop thinking about them as people and they just become jobs. It's you or it's them. If you think any harder than that, you'll drive yourself crazy."

"I think it might be too late for that," Dallas said, his voice small.

"You're not crazy." I kissed his mouth softly. "You've had a difficult afternoon, that's all." I wished I'd known how close we were to him when we were at Flirts. We could have saved him from a couple of hours of self torment.

"Why did you come here specifically?" Atlas asked. "Why the change room in the pool area?"

Dallas frowned at him. "I don't know. I don't know how I got in here." He glanced around himself.

"You must have let yourself in with the key card," Storm said.

"I suppose so," Dallas said. "I don't remember anything after I threw the knife away."

"Did you drive?" I asked. "Storm said your car wasn't in the car park." The idea of him driving in the state he was in was terrifying. For him and for anyone else on the road.

Dallas' mouth opened and closed a couple of times. "I don't remember. I don't think so. I wasn't in a fit state to drive."

"We better find your car," Frost said. "And bring it back here before someone realises it's anywhere near Flirts."

I winced. "Good idea. We don't want anything leading anyone here." Which reminded me of earlier when I'd thought we were being watched. Had they seen him leave the club with a knife? Was there anyone there in the first place? Or was my paranoia getting the better of me?

"I'm sorry," Dallas whispered. "I've fucked all of this up." He sounded devastated. Full of self-loathing.

I brushed a hand over his temple. "You didn't

fuck anything up. If you hadn't stayed to listen to India, you wouldn't have known what she was up to. If you hadn't done what you did, she would have run off and told what she knew. She would have exposed you and Ramsey, and the rest of us. You listened to your gut."

"Some might say you're a hero," Frost said.

"I hate to admit it," Storm crouched down again, "if it was me, I would have said what Ramsey told me I should say, then left. It wouldn't have crossed my mind that she'd do something behind my back. I would have gone off and cuddled puppies without a fucking clue."

"Me too," Frost said. "But you didn't. I think you're fucking epic." He pulled Dallas in for a hug.

"Frost is right, you're epic." I waited until Frost let him go before giving Dallas a hug too. He wasn't trembling anymore. His body felt firm and strong, buoyed by our confidence in him.

"Thank you," he said, looking around at all of us. "Anyone else in the world would have said I was a complete fuck up."

"If they say that to you, they can answer to my fist," Storm growled.

"Mine too," Frost agreed.

"And mine," Atlas said.

"Mine too," Jay said over Atlas' shoulder.

"I'm not sure if I'd use a fist, but they'd answer to me too," I said. "I guess we better find out who Nile Fox is."

Hopefully by then they would have found the knife and Dallas' car, and covered any tracks he left behind.

Chapter Eight

Chelsea

Ramsey stood in front of the kitchen island like he was a coach delivering a motivational speech to the team. He walked through the door like nothing happened and waited for us all to settle down and listen.

"I feel like I'm back at school again," Frost whispered loudly. "Anyone got any paper for a spitball?"

As one, we all turned to look at him.

Jay choked back a laugh.

Storm shook his head and gestured for Ramsey to go ahead.

Ramsey didn't seem bothered by the comment. If anything, he seemed to be holding back a laugh of his own.

"Dallas' car is back in the garage. The knife was

dealt with. The scene was cleaned. It'll be ruled a tragic accident. Divina has agreed to the story I gave her. She wants to avoid scrutiny. To the best of my knowledge, the only other people who saw anything are sitting right here. No reason for anyone to know anything else."

Those were more words than I'd heard him say since we met. In typical Ramsey style, he was concise and to the point. He didn't waste a single word.

"Thank you," Dallas said. He sat in a chair nursing a bottle of beer. I hadn't seen him take more than a couple of sips, but he looked better than when we first found him.

Ramsey gave him a nod. "Yep."

"What about Otis Skinner?" Atlas stood with his shoulder leaning against the window. Jay sat in a chair beside him, arms crossed. They stayed close to each other since we got back up to the apartment.

"He's pissed," Ramsey said. "India was giving him information on customers of Flirts. And staff, including former staff." He slid me a glance and tipped his head forward slightly.

"That was how Dominic King knew I used to work there," I said softly.

"She might have been the one who told Bruce Fergus," Frost suggested.

"If that's the case, I'm glad she's dead," Storm said. "Good job, Tex." He reached over to thump Dallas' back.

"Thanks," Dallas said, his chin almost touching his chest. He didn't look as happy about it as Storm did.

"Divina would probably thank you too," I said. "Talking about customers like that was a huge breach of trust. Not to mention her NDA. She promises everyone complete discretion from the moment they walk through the door, to the moment they leave again. If any of them found out people knew they frequented the club, they'd never go there again. Without regular customers, the place would go out of business. India knew that."

"India was looking out for India," Storm said. "If she was being paid so well she could give up working there, she wouldn't care if she set the place on fire before she walked away."

"Exactly," Frost agreed. "If Dallas hadn't killed her, someone else would have, to keep her quiet."

"It sounds to me like it was too late for that," I said, exhaling heavily. "Who knows what information she shared and who she shared it with, other than Otis Skinner?"

"Or who he might have shared it to," Atlas said. "We know about Dominic King, but who else? This Nile Fox guy? Carlos Jones?"

"Wouldn't rule out any of them," Ramsey said. "Blackmail material, especially if they're powerful people in Dusk Bay." He lifted an eyebrow in my direction.

"Lots of them are," I said. "But you know I can't discuss it." I owed Divina that much.

"Give me a list," Ramsey said. "I need to know who's potentially being blackmailed. So we can stop it. And find who's doing the blackmailing."

I swiped my tongue over my lip. "Doing that would be a breach of their privacy."

"It'll stop King from becoming more powerful," Ramsey countered. "Carlos Jones too. I don't want to insist."

"By insist you mean threaten, right?" Storm took a few steps towards Ramsey, hands curled into fists.

Ramsey stood his ground. "It's important. Might even keep us alive."

Storm glared at him, but then glanced at me, uncertain as to whether he should beat the shit out of Ramsey or back off a bit. For once, he wasn't jumping in feet first, without looking. Whether that was because he liked Ramsey, or because he was uncertain of the situation, I wasn't sure. Possibly both. Either way, the hesitation spoke volumes.

I rubbed the heel of my hand over my forehead. "If you promise the list won't get past you or anyone who absolutely needs to know. And if you promise no one will know where it came from." I felt bad enough agreeing to it without Divina knowing I stabbed her through the heart. Figuratively, of course.

"Promise," Ramsey said. "It sucks, but it's necessary."

Storm and Frost exchanged glances before Frost said, "Storm and I could add to that list. I saw a few influential people when I was there."

"Me too," Dallas said reluctantly.

Ramsey nodded. "Whatever you've got."

"Can we be sure the Brantley family won't use that list to bribe those people instead?" Jay asked.

"Better us than the other side," Ramsey said.

I wasn't sure if I believed that, but there was nothing I could do to stop it from happening. Not unless I kept my mouth shut. If doing that risked anyone in this room, what choice did I have?

"This is getting messy," I said, weary.

At this point, it didn't matter where we went, we had to be on alert. Storm's apartment might be the only place we could truly relax and be ourselves, without being on guard every single moment.

Although, if I was honest with myself, I was a little on edge here too. If anyone really wanted to get at us, there was no reason they wouldn't try to reach us here. Whether they'd succeed or not was another thing, but they might take the chance.

"It's been messy for a long time," Atlas said. "That's why Jay and I are here."

"What will it take to not be messy?" Dallas asked.

"Us dealing with the major players before they deal with us," Atlas said. "But we can't just run in there and end them all."

"Why not?" Frost asked. He seemed to like the idea.

"Because it could get us dead," Atlas said firmly. "And we don't know for sure if Carlos Jones is involved. We don't know who Nile Fox is. We could kill a few people, then have a shit ton more come after us. If you're down for that, then go ahead. I'll be the one saying I told you so at your funeral. If they can find your body."

"We need to know who and what we're dealing

with," Ramsey agreed. "The boss might not want us dealing with anything."

"That too," Atlas agreed. "We need to sit tight and wait for orders."

Frost huffed. "I guess I can do that."

"Of course you can," I told him. "It's not as though you don't have a season to focus on. Remember football?" I managed a smile along with the light tease.

He made a show of scratching his temple. "It rings a bell. Something about a ball and feet." He dropped his hand in a 'who knows,' gesture.

Storm rolled his eyes. "You're an idiot." He spoke with affection. No one could doubt the feelings between the two of them had grown. They were closer now than they'd ever been, and I was here for it.

"You still love me." Frost grinned.

"Yeah, maybe," Storm said. "You're all right."

"I'm better than all right and you know it," Frost said. "Everyone in this room knows how awesome I am." He gestured around to all of us.

"Of course we do," I said. "You're the awesomest. We all are."

"Team Awesomest for the win," he declared. He leaned over to offer Jay a fist bump.

Jay smiled and returned the gesture. They

seemed to be getting more and more comfortable with each other.

I supposed both of them fucking me at the same time would bond guys together. What would it be like with all six of them? Messy, but I wanted to anyway. Hearing all of them groaning and grunting, thrusting and sweating at the same time would be memorable, to say the least. My clit throbbed eagerly at the idea of it.

I caught Atlas' eye and grinned. Seeing them getting along for a change was gratifying. How long would it last? That was anyone's guess, but I'd enjoy it while it did.

Atlas grinned back. He was way too adorable for his own good. They all were.

All of them were so different and yet here we all were, together. Sharing this space and taking care of each other. Joking around, even when the situation was dark. People could be out there right now, wanting us dead, but we had each other's backs.

"Are you going to get T-shirts and make us wear them?" Storm grumbled. "Team Fucking Awesomest." The look he gave Frost was bordering on the evil eye. Somewhere between disgust and 'don't you fucking dare.'

Frost snapped his fingers. "I wasn't going to, but

now you mention it, that's a good idea. We'd all look adorable in matching T-shirts. Or better yet, matching jackets."

"Don't forget the matching socks," Jay said.

"And hats," Atlas said, giving Storm a sideways look, knowing he'd get the other man going. "Maybe track pants with the team name down the leg. And matching duffel bags."

Storm shook his head. "You're a fucking nightmare. You won't be done until we all look like idiots."

I wasn't sure who he directed the comment at, but there was no heat behind his words. He might even wear the outfit with pride.

"I wouldn't mind a duffel bag," Jay said. "Those are useful."

"I could put my medical equipment in one," I said. "But I'd settle for a Dusk Bay Smashers bag instead." People would stare if I had a bag with Team Awesomest written down the side. They'd stare harder if I had a matching outfit.

Storm pointed a finger at me. "Finally, some common sense. I already have all the shit for our team. Including the socks."

"What about the underwear?" Frost teased.

"There is no fucking Smashers underwear," Storm said. He looked almost horrified at the idea.

As though merchandise underwear wasn't already a thing in the world. As if he didn't wear boxers with superhero characters on them. Not often, but I'd seen him in them once or twice. It was a cute look on him.

"*Yet*," Frost said ominously. "I'm going to suggest that to Coach tomorrow. Storm will be first in line to buy some."

"Sounds like you'll be first in line," Jay said to Frost.

"I would be, but I'll hide behind Storm, so he can be first," Frost said. "Or I could hide behind you, so you can be second."

"Now they're arguing over who is going to be first and second in line to buy underwear," Storm complained to Atlas.

Atlas chuckled. "What next? Smashers watch bands?"

"Now that's something I'd like," Storm said thoughtfully. "It would go with my phone case."

"You have a Smashers phone case?" Atlas frowned.

"Shit, yeah, I do." Storm leaned forward to pull out his phone and show the case to the other guy.

Atlas looked impressed. "That's sick, bro. I'm going to have to get one for myself."

"Now you're part of the team," Frost said.

"Exactly." Atlas nodded. "Since I'm one of us, I might as well look like it. Does that come in different colours?" He nodded towards the phone case. "Wouldn't want to get ours mixed up."

I leaned back against Frost while they talked about phone cases and other random team merchandise. For a while, the fear and death were put aside. Not forgotten, but not at the forefront of the conversation, giving us all a chance to breathe.

For now.

Chapter Nine

Chelsea

UNABLE TO SLEEP, I SLIPPED OUT OF BED AND walked as quietly as I could to the kitchen for a drink of water.

Glass in hand, I stepped through the living room and over to the window that overlooked Dusk Bay. The lights of the city twinkled, reflecting on the expanse of water that disappeared into the horizon.

"This is all a lot, isn't it?" Ramsey's voice was soft in the otherwise silent space.

I startled and turned around, almost spilling my water all over me. I'd missed the dark shape that sat in an armchair facing the window. Fortunately for me, he was friend, not foe.

"Sorry, didn't mean to scare you." He pushed himself to his feet and closed the gap between us.

"You're lucky I wasn't one of the guys," I said. "They might have struck out first and asked questions later."

He chuckled. "Nothing I couldn't deal with. I knew it was you. No offence, you're not built like a professional men's rugby player."

"No, I'm built more like a professional *women's* rugby player," I said. I took a sip of my drink and turned back to the view.

"Exactly." He moved around behind me and began to massage my shoulders. "Strong, fast and capable."

"I don't feel very strong or capable lately." I dropped my chin and enjoyed the way his hands felt, working out the knots in my muscles.

"You should," he said. "Plenty of people would have come apart after everything that's happened. Not you. You held it together. Held everyone else together too."

"I think you might be giving me more credit than I deserve," I said. "We've all worked together to keep each other more or less sane. If it wasn't for all of you, I would have lost my shit a long time ago."

"You're including me in that," he stated.

"Should I not?" I asked over my shoulder.

"You definitely should," he said. "I'm all in on this too. With you. With the other guys."

"With the other guys as in..." I didn't want to push him, but I was curious.

"Friends," he said quickly. "Brothers. The only one I want is you. Romantically. Physically."

"I know they'll respect that, and so will I," I said. I didn't expect them all to be into each other. As long as they were happy, that was all that mattered.

"Of course." He took the empty glass from my hand and put it aside before turning me to face him. "I said I was going to claim you."

"Yes, you did." My heart skipped a couple of times. "Are you going to do that now?"

He grabbed a fistful of my hair and tilted my head back. "Yes. I'm going to make you mine now. Get on your knees." He pushed me down, his fingers still tangled in my hair.

His face was illuminated by the lights coming through the window. His gaze locked on me.

I kept my eyes on his and sank to my knees. He wore only loose track pants, which barely concealed his rapidly growing erection.

"Take out my cock." His voice was already strained with need.

I pushed down the front of his pants and found

he'd gone commando. His cock popped out in front of my nose, thick and hard, vein pulsing underneath my fingertips.

"It really is the quiet ones," I said, admiring the line of four piercings decorating his cock. I wouldn't have figured him for a Jacob's ladder guy, but it was perfection on him. Without it, his cock would have been a work of art. With it... I was desperate to feel him inside me.

"I like to keep people guessing," he said. "Open your mouth." He tapped his head against my lips.

I opened, taking him all the way down to the back of my throat.

He groaned. "Yeah, just like that." One hand holding me in place, he slid out slowly before pushing all the way back in. Hips rolling, he thrust in and out of me, fucking my mouth while I sucked and ran my tongue up and down his piercings, making him harder still.

With a moan, he wrenched himself out of my mouth. "Clothes off."

Still on my knees, I wriggled out of my sleep shorts and singlet, kneeling naked in front of him. At the same time, he pushed his track pants off and stepped out of them.

"Stand up." He grabbed my hand, pulled me to

my feet and turned me to face the window. "Bend over." He pushed my upper body forward, my weight on my hands, palms pressed against the cool window.

Gripping my hips, positioned his cock outside my entrance before sliding in with one smooth stroke.

I cried out at the suddenness of his penetration and the exquisiteness of his piercings which massaged me all the way through. His cock was so thick already. With the hard bars across his length, I felt everything. So full, so spoilt.

"So tight." He stood still, savouring the way I felt around him.

"You feel so good," I whispered. "Fuck me hard."

He grabbed my hair again and pulled my head back. "Let's get this straight. I give the orders. You obey."

I shivered deliciously. "Yes, sir," I whispered. "I'll obey."

"Yes, you will." He let go of my hair and gripped my hip again. "I will fuck you hard, because I want to." He pulled all the way out and slammed hard into me. So hard it hurt, just the way I liked it.

I moaned. "Fuck, yes."

He thrust several more times, each harder than

the last. So hard I almost couldn't take it, but I did. I wanted to. Each and every thrust.

"Chelsea..." He pulled out of me, turned me around again and pressed my back against the window. He hooked a hand under one of my knees and raised my leg so he could thrust back into me. "You're mine now. Mine. Say it."

"I'm yours," I said breathlessly. I was so close to coming it was almost impossible to think. All I knew was his cock sliding in and out of my body.

"Who owns you?" he half-whispered, half-moaned.

"You do," I panted. "You own me."

Luckily Storm didn't appear just in time to refute that. As far as I was concerned, they all owned me. And I owned all of them. All six of my guys.

"Yes, I do," he said. "Come for me." He meant right then and there. Whether I thought my body was ready or not. He was expecting me to do exactly what he told me to do, when he told me to do it.

I promised to obey, so I did. The words barely passed his lips when I came hard around his cock. I saw stars in distant galaxies, felt nothing but bliss and the man inside me, pounding into me with rough, even strokes. Using my body the way I liked to be used.

"So obedient," he said approvingly. "You're going to let me come inside you now. You're going to take every drop of my cum."

"Yes, please," I begged. At that moment, there was nothing more I wanted in this world than to have him come inside my body. To feel his release trickle back out of me. To know that there was absolutely nothing between us. To have him claim me fully like he said he would.

He grunted and thrust several more times before his fingers dug into my leg and he gave in to the orgasm that surged through him. He thrust faster until his hot release exploded inside me, filling me with warmth and stealing another orgasm from me.

I didn't know it was coming until it ripped through me, making me scream out his name, and beg him never to stop fucking me.

Finally, we both came back down, puffing and slick with sweat.

"So good," he said, half to himself. "Your body was made for me. Same as mine was made for you."

"Did you get the piercings for me?" I asked as he lowered my leg back down.

"Didn't know it at the time, but yeah," he said. "Just for you." He wrapped his arms around me and pulled me flush against him. "You're everything."

I snuggled against him, inhaling the unique scent of him, enhanced by the sweat we'd worked up together. "I'm a lucky girl."

He kissed the top of my head. "I'm the lucky one." After a moment he added, "And anyone watching through the window."

I looked over my shoulder. If anyone was watching, I couldn't see them. I didn't mind if they saw everything. It wasn't as though people hadn't seen me fuck dozens of times before. This freebie was just for them. And for Ramsey and me.

"I'm sure they enjoyed the show." I turned back to him.

"Without doubt. Time to clean up. You'll have a shower with me." Like before, he wasn't asking, he was telling.

And, like before, I hurried to obey, knowing he wasn't done with me yet.

Chapter Ten

Chelsea

"How are you settling in?" Doctor Stuart lowered himself into the seat beside me and reached for the sides of his seatbelt.

"I'm loving it," I said sincerely. As long as I kept a relatively safe distance from Otis Skinner and focused on my job, I was in my element. "It's everything I thought it would be and more."

"It's certainly more." He clicked his seatbelt and adjusted the sash across his waist. "Ever since I've done this, it's always been more." He glanced over at me and smiled.

"I'm here for it," I said. "The guys are great and the travel is amazing." The *waiting* to travel part was less than thrilling, but the rest was a blur of excitement. Watching the guys train, then travelling to watch them play, was dream come true stuff.

"I remember having your youthful enthusiasm," he said. "I still have the enthusiasm, but it's not so youthful anymore." He chuckled.

I scoffed gently. "You're not that old. You can keep up with everything as well as I can."

"Maybe not quite as well," he said. "I've learnt how to pace myself in a way that looks like I'm keeping up. Don't look too closely, or you'll see the truth." He winked at me.

"I've been watching very closely and you're keeping up just fine," I told him. "You will be for lots more years to come." At least, I hoped that was the case.

As far as I knew, he was one of the few truly innocent people around me. Either I was mistaken, or he really was oblivious to the real nature of Dusk Bay, and risked getting caught in the firing line by being around the rest of us.

I wasn't joking when I said I watched him closely. It wasn't just professional interest and the desire to learn, it was concern for his safety. Ruthless people didn't give a shit who they stepped on to get where they wanted to go. If he stood in their way, he'd be dead.

"Maybe," he said. "I'll be retiring in a couple of years. Then I won't need to worry about keeping up with anyone but my wife. Trust me, she's enough of a handful when she wants to be." He made a face, but his eyes were still smiling, the laugh lines around them crinkling.

"I'm sure she'd say the same about you," I teased.

He chuckled. "Without doubt." He glanced past me out the window as the plane taxied towards the runway. "It doesn't matter how many times I do it, sitting on a plane while it takes off never gets old. Of course, by the time we get there, I'm glad to feel it land too. Travelling with the Wallabies is even more exhausting than this. That's when you realise they're right when they say Australia is far away. Especially when travelling to the UK."

"I'll bet," I replied. "It must be a challenge to keep a team of bored footy players in line during a long haul flight." The national rugby team would be a handful at times, like any group of professional athletes.

"When the alcohol starts flowing, it is," Doctor Stuart agreed. "Manners tend to go out the window. More than once I've seen them streak naked through the middle of an aircraft. The flight crew was not impressed. Okay, some of them were, but others not so much."

I grinned, but hoped none of my guys would do that. If I had to guess which one of them would, my money would be on Frost. He was the most likely to let himself go, and get into trouble midair. Especially if someone dared him or made him a wager.

"I don't think Coach Stanley would be too happy about that either," I said. I rested my elbow on the armrest and watched the ground fall away underneath us.

"Probably not," Doctor Stuart agreed. "They'd issue some hefty fines for misbehaviour, especially for what they do while intoxicated. Nothing the boys couldn't handle, I suppose, given their salaries. Although, if people didn't record everything on their phones for posterity, the players might not remember having done it. Nowadays, the team drinking on aircraft is frowned upon, so they tend to be better behaved. Or if they're not, at least they can watch it back afterwards." He chuckled to himself.

I glanced forward between the seats, to the front of the plane where the guys sat. Today, it seemed less likely that Storm and Atlas would get into a fist fight midair. That would be worse than them running naked through the plane. Much worse, if I was honest.

It wouldn't bother me if the whole team walked around naked. They'd already been half-naked, stripping off their suits and changing into T-shirts and track pants. I don't mind admitting I was happy to watch them do it. I had a keen appreciation for the naked, muscular, male form. That was another perk of this job.

"You must have seen all sorts of interesting things over the years," I said.

"Two hundred percent," he agreed. "Everything from Tabasco sauce in water bottles, to tomato sauce packets hidden in boots. I've seen glitter come out of places it shouldn't have been in the first place. I'm still not sure how it got there." He made a face. "I've seen teams celebrate their wins when it looked like they were going to lose badly. And I've seen them drown their sorrows when the game didn't go their way."

He sighed softly. "I've seen the most harmless-looking tackle lead to career ending injuries. I've seen grown men sob when they realised they'd never play football again. And I've seen the young rookies come through, terrified they'd let themselves and the team down, but excited to be given the chance. Their first game out there on the field is always memorable. You know what they say, you never forget your first time."

I didn't think that was intended to be a football reference, but I nodded anyway.

"That's why I wanted to do this. To help prevent career-ending injuries and to be here for the highs and lows. It's one thing to sit in the crowd and watch, but it's another to be a part of it. To know you're making a difference in people's lives. Inspiring the next generation and all that."

He smiled softly. "Look at us getting all sentimental. It's true though. The ups and downs, the ins and outs, that's what we live for. Every single person on this aircraft is here for the same reason. For the team and the fans. Because this is what we love more than anything. And some of us get paid well to do it." He smirked in the direction of the players in front of us.

"Considering they put their bodies on the line every time they get out of bed, they deserve to be paid well," I said.

Every game could be their last. The money they made might have to keep them for the rest of their lives. If they had the sense to save it, and not spend it all on fuck knows what. The same could be said for anyone though, not just professional athletes.

"Otherwise they might not get out of bed," he said jokingly.

"It's a good incentive," I said.

I knew how much hard work went into a job that required a lot of physical effort, and I was paid well for it too. Dancing in heels was even more athletic than playing football. In some ways, I missed it. Not so much the stilettos. Those I didn't miss even slightly. My feet were happy in lower heels, thank you very much. The rest of it though, I loved it on most nights. I was strong, fit and powerful. There were worse ways to put myself through university.

Doctor Stuart flipped open his tray table and placed his laptop onto it. "This is a good opportunity to get some work done."

"Good idea." I got out my own laptop and opened it. "How do you think the guys will go tomorrow night? They were training well this morning."

"They were," he agreed. "That's the first time I've seen Storm Keller and Atlas Underwood communicate with each other. If they play like that, they'll smash the opposition. It's about time they sorted themselves out." He glanced over at me. "Did you have anything to do with that?"

"I might have," I said carefully. "I've been encouraging them to be nicer to each other. The other guys have as well. Jay and Frost in particular. Dallas and Ramsey have had a hand in it too, though."

Finding Dallas in the change area the way they had seemed to have flipped a switch with them. Some people bonded over a mutual appreciation for cake. Others bonded over finding a devastated teammate who'd just killed a woman. Whatever it took.

Doctor Stuart's eyebrows rose. "Unless I'm mistaken, I count six."

"That's right," I said lightly. "They care about me and some of them care about each other. It's complicated, but we're making it work."

"Huh, how about that," he said softly. "Well, if the guys play better for it, then it has to be a good thing."

"If they play worse because of it, we can both get in line to kick their asses." I smiled. "After they're done kicking each other's."

Doctor Stuart chuckled. "I can picture that, yes. They're passionate about the team. They wouldn't let much get in their way. And now they have a pretty woman to keep them in line, they'll do even better."

"Not the whole team," I said dryly.

"Just the single ones," he said slowly.

"Not even all the single ones," I protested. "I left a

few for the other women in the world." Six was enough for me. I had no interest in adding to that number. Not unless it was a puppy or a kitten. Maybe one of each for each guy.

"As long as it doesn't impact your work either," Doctor Stuart said. "Then I wish you all the best." He gave me a meaningful look, like he'd be the first to step in and tell me if I wasn't doing what I should be doing. Of course he would; he was my supervisor. I wouldn't want him to see me doing the wrong thing and let it slide for any reason. That was a really good way to get into bad habits, and I didn't need that. It wasn't good for me and it wasn't good for the team.

"I won't let it do that," I assured him. "Thank you for your support. Other people might think it's... weird." Not that I gave two hoots what other people thought. I didn't care how they chose to live their lives.

"I'll be completely honest with you, I've seen many weird things in my day," he said. "This doesn't even make the top ten. If I was a younger man, I might look into all of this myself. I'm sure my wife would love five more boyfriends." He smiled softly.

Clearly her and her needs were important to him. That was sweet. The world needed more men like that.

"You're never too old to have extra boyfriends," I said.

I sensed he and his wife were in for an interesting conversation when he got home. Whether it led to anything or not was another story. There was certainly nothing wrong with considering it. As long as everyone was happy and communicated with each other, then they should go for it.

"That sounds like a bumper sticker," he said. "One would certainly raise some eyebrows."

"I'll look into having those made," I said jokingly.

After Frost had Team Awesomest bumper stickers printed. Hopefully he was joking about that. I didn't want to get out of work after a long day, to find my car covered in them. I could picture him doing just that. Bright, glittery stickers all over my vehicle. Of course, he'd cover everyone else's cars with them too.

I made a note to keep a close eye on him so he didn't pull a prank like that. Stickers weren't good for the paint on cars, as far as I knew.

Doctor Stuart chuckled and bent over his laptop to get to work.

I watched the coastline disappear before I did the same.

Chapter Eleven

Chelsea

"Where are we going?"

As soon as the game finished, Ramsey bundled me into a car and started driving out of Auckland. When none of the guys objected, except to give Ramsey warning looks, I assumed they must have worked something out beforehand.

I didn't know how I felt about them going behind my back, but if they trusted him to take me wherever we were going, I'd roll with it.

Admittedly, Storm looked less than impressed and Dallas slightly strained, but they let me go anyway. After Storm quietly growled to Ramsey that he better fucking look after me or he'd have him to answer to.

"You'll see." Ramsey had a stubborn set to his jaw

that clearly said there was no point in pushing, he wasn't going to tell me a thing until he was ready.

What was it with these men? And why did I like it so much?

I crossed my arms and leaned back to doze against the seat while we navigated virtually empty roads. This part of New Zealand was a lot quieter than Dusk Bay.

Hopefully safer too.

We drove in silence until we reached a small campground on the east coast of the north island. He led me to a tent set apart from the others and we had a few hours' sleep.

The sun wasn't even up yet when he gently shook me awake.

"What?" I asked sleepily.

I was comfortable where I was, rolled up in blankets. I'd been having a nice dream that involved not having to worry about people chasing us and trying to kill us.

I snuggled back down, wanting to let sleep claim me again. Why did I have to like a man who'd wake me from the beautiful dream? I should have known he had a sadistic streak; why else would I be attracted to him? I must be a masochist or something. Unless he was planning to fuck me. That I'd wake up for. I had a feeling that wasn't what was about, worse luck.

"Come on, sleepyhead," he coaxed. "It'll be worth it." He slipped out of the tent and waited until I dressed before we were back in the car driving down an empty road.

After a few kilometres, we turned off into a darkened location. The headlights only illuminated some kind of small building and another couple of cars parked outside.

Exactly the kind of place my brother would take someone to torture or kill them.

Should I run when I got the chance? Maybe, but I knew I could trust him, even in a place like this.

I hoped to hell my instincts were right. Otherwise, I was fucked.

"What is this place?" I rubbed my eyes.

Lights came on, gradually illuminating a small airfield, with an office, a couple of hangers and a few light aircraft.

"We're not going to jump out of a plane, are we? It's too early in the morning." I'd have to work up to something like that. Right then, I was too sleepy.

On the other hand, I wouldn't be able to overthink it too much. Plus, if it was still dark, I wouldn't be able to see how high up we were. I suspected that defeated the purpose of skydiving, but what did I know?

"We're not going on a plane," he said. He got out of the car and walked around to open my door. Not just because he was being a gentleman, but because I was frozen in my seat, staring out the windscreen.

As if to punctuate his words, a flash lit up the predawn morning. I flinched until I realised what it was. A burst of heat to inflate a hot air balloon.

"You didn't?" I tore my eyes away from the balloon for long enough to glance questioningly at him. I let him take my hand and tug me out of the car.

"Yep, I did." He laced his fingers in mine and let me over to the basket.

"Perfect morning for it," the balloonist said cheerfully. He was one of the bad guys, obviously. Surely only evil people were cheerful when the sun hadn't even come up yet. Right? I didn't mind mornings, but I wasn't a fan of 'early as fuck.' This was even earlier than that.

"Are you sure this is safe?" I eyed the basket doubtfully. I'd never been this close to a hot air balloon before. Now I was, I realised there wasn't much between us and the ground. Just a flimsy basket, the side low enough that I could fall out if I wasn't careful.

Or if I was pushed.

"Better be," Ramsey growled. He eyed the basket like it should be the strongest basket in history, or else. Or else what, I didn't know. The basket didn't seem particularly intimidated.

"It's perfectly safe," the balloonist said. According to the embroidered stitches on the breast of his shirt, his name was Gavin. "I've done this a million times. You're going to have a ball. Get on in, your breakfast is on board already. We want to be away before the sun rises."

Ballooning in the dark didn't seem all that safe to me, but Ramsey tugged me toward the basket and inside.

I stood away from the edge, even though we hadn't left the ground yet. I'd have to work up to getting any closer to the side. Or better yet, I could stay here, where it was safe.

Another man moved to untie the basket from where it was tethered to the ground and we slowly lifted off, into the air.

Tentatively, I peered over the side of the basket. "Are you sure this is a good idea?"

"This is one of the first places in the world to see

the sunrise," Ramsey said. "We're going to see it in style." He handed me a glass of champagne when Gavin poured them for us.

"I wouldn't have picked you for a romantic," I admitted. I clinked my glass lightly on his and took a sip.

"I'm not usually. For the right person..." Glass held carefully in one hand, he tangled his fingers in my hair and pulled me in for a kiss.

"That's so sweet." He tasted of sparkling wine and mint, having brushed his teeth before we left the campground.

"You're sweet." He snaked an arm around my waist and pulled me to him, facing us both to the east.

The ocean sparkled in front of us, golden with the first rays of the morning sun. Gradually, the sky turned yellow, then pink, before that gave way to blue.

This was going to be a glorious day and here we were, floating above the ground, seeing it begin.

Gavin served us breakfast of croissants, fruit and yoghurt while we admired the view, and enjoyed each other's company. Like always, Ramsey didn't say much, but he conveyed a lot from glances and brushes of his hand over my cheek, and the occasional kiss.

I could almost forget Gavin was there, operating the balloon. He stayed behind us, quiet and discreet. Letting us enjoy the beautiful morning.

"This was worth getting up early for," I said with a sigh. The ocean was spread out in front of us, and the stunning green landscape behind. We floated over valleys dotted with houses, and beaches and inlets.

"Told you," Ramsey said, looking smug.

I shoved my shoulder into his arm. "What if you were wrong?"

He scoffed. "I'm never wrong. Anyway, I knew you'd like this. It's calm."

"I certainly needed some calm after the last few weeks," I agreed. This was so relaxing, I could have happily stayed here for hours. Frankly, the idea of getting on a plane and going back to Australia, back to reality, sucked.

"Me too," he agreed.

I slid him a glance. Everything that was going on, he'd been dealing with it for longer than the other guys. Maybe even longer than Atlas and Jay. Yes, I knew about the dark side of Dusk Bay, but he'd lived it. He needed this break as much as I did, possibly more.

"You think anyone would notice if we bought one of those cottages down there and ran away?" I gestured towards the ground with my champagne glass.

"Yes, but it's tempting," he said ruefully. His gaze lingered on a cottage as we floated past. If he had a parachute, he might jump down and never be seen again. If there were two parachutes, I might follow him.

"It really is," I said softly. "But we'd both miss the team and our families."

"Unless it's a seven bedroom house," he said.

"Frost would love that." I smiled, picturing the expression on his face. I didn't know how he'd feel about living in New Zealand, but he'd love the idea of a house big enough for all of us.

"Maybe we can find something like that when we get home. Something away from the city and all the craziness." A big sprawling house on a hundred acres sounded right to me. No neighbours nearby to bother us. We could scream and shout, and play music as loud as we liked. We could fuck in every room and all over the property if we wanted to. No one would be there to see it but us.

"I'm in," Ramsey said.

"Me too. Now we just have to convince Storm." He was very attached to his apartment. Or maybe it was the idea that the space was his and we just lived in it. Someday, he'd have to accept that a space was ours, not just his.

"He can come, or get left behind," Ramsey said dryly. "That'll convince him."

I laughed softly. "Good point. He won't want to be left out." I could just imagine his irritation when he thought that might happen. We'd earn some of his best glares.

Ramsey chuckled. "Nope." He held me closer as the balloon started to descend, back towards the airfield.

"This was perfect," I said with a sigh. "Thank you."

He kissed my temple. "Of course. Anything for my beautiful woman." Before I could respond to that, he said, "I fell for you the moment I saw you." He rested the side of his head against mine and exhaled softly. Once again, saying more without words than he ever did with them.

"You intrigued me," I said. "You're not loud like some of the others. You're quiet, but intense."

"That's me," he said simply, silently owning the moment.

"I could fall for you," I told him.

"You're not getting rid of me either way," he said. "You're mine."

The words sent shivers up and down my spine every time he said them. In the very best way. How did I get so lucky?

Sure, life was hectic and dangerous, but these six guys, who all cared for me... I was still trying to get my head around it. Six gorgeous men who wanted to share the rest of their lives with me. Somehow, I managed to score the jackpot.

"I don't want to get rid of you," I told him. "You're mine too."

"Yours," he whispered. "Always."

We held each other as the balloon slowed and bumped gently back to the ground.

"Then we go, folks," Gavin said. "Another perfect sunrise here in Aotearoa." The local's preferred name for New Zealand.

"Thank you," I told him as Ramsey helped me out of the basket. "It was lovely."

Gavin nodded and hurried to secure the basket to the ground. "Any time, folks."

I laced my fingers in Ramsey's and we headed back to the car. Back to Auckland and the airport.

Back to reality.

Fuck.

Chapter Twelve

Atlas

I STOOD, BALANCED ON THE BALLS OF MY FEET, watching the boys form a scrum. Adrenaline roared through me. Anticipation.

Watching, waiting.

Finally, our side had possession of the ball. A blink of an eye later, it was passed to the fly half, who passed it to me. I took off at a run, slamming my way through the defensive line. I'd hurt later, but right now, I didn't feel a thing but the thrill of the impact. Shoving guys back and forcing my way through.

They held up, giving me no choice but to pass the ball back behind me.

The crowd roared, screaming and shouting. Thousands of voices chanting in time to the throb of blood through my ears.

"Smashers! Smashers! Smashers!"

Nothing in the world was like a home crowd to drive you on. Like me, they loved a good, hard game, and we were giving it to them. They adored us for it.

I swiped a hand over my forehead, wiping sweat away before it trickled into my eyes.

This was what I fucking loved, playing this brutal game. This, right here, was the best fucking job on the face of the planet. Every time I stepped out on the field, every time I brought down an opposition player, slamming them into the grass, my blood sang.

I was a warrior, this was my battle. We'd fight until the bitter end, giving it everything. Blood, sweat and tears.

Brent Evans, usually known as Frog for some reason that was lost in time, caught the ball and bolted down the field, running like he was navigating a maze. The opposition tried to stop him, but he darted around them, brushed them off and threw himself over the try line. He slid almost a metre across the grass before coming to a stop, the ball held out in front of him.

No one in the stadium would doubt that was a try. And a fucking well-executed one too. They'd show that on replay for the next couple of days.

"Fuck yeah." I grinned. I glanced at the clock. From the start of the game, the opposition was never going to catch us and now they were out of time.

Three.

Two.

One.

The horn sounded, signalling the end of the game.

Another win for the Dusk Bay Smashers. We were dominating this season, but we hadn't played the Sydney Devils yet, and they hadn't lost a game. When we met, that would change. My loyalty was here now. I'd help my team claim victory and let the Devils taste defeat.

I trotted over to the guys and threw myself into a group hug with anyone who was close enough. I found myself with Jay on one side of me and Frost on the other. Storm was on the other side of him and Ramsey and Dallas on the other side of Jay. Maybe the hug wasn't so random after all. We were drawn to each other like a packet of magnets. Of course, Storm was the negative and I was the positive.

"Good job," I said to all of them. "We fucking destroyed them." Winning never got old. It was the biggest rush there was, second only to a good fuck. Priorities.

"Fuck yeah we did," Frost agreed. "If they're not careful, we'll win the whole damn thing."

"No reason we can't," Storm said. Blood caked the side of his face, mingling with dirt. He'd taken a few hard hits. The rest of us had too. We left nothing on the table. Not one of us held back a thing. We'd played better together than we ever had before. If we kept going like this, we'd be unbeatable.

When we kept going like this, I corrected myself.

"I need a shower," Jay said. He was the first to back out of the hug, gave the crowd a brief wave and trotted to the locker room. His back was stiff, a sure sign he'd had enough of the noise and crowds and needed to step away.

"Me too." I followed close behind. Not too close to crowd him, but close enough to be supportive and to keep anyone else from getting too close. Making myself a barricade between him and the rest of the world. Until he was ready to deal with it again.

He barely stepped into the locker room before he was tearing off his shoes and socks. He carried them the rest of the way to his locker before dropping them and starting to strip off. He was always in a hurry to get everything off his feet, but when he was overwhelmed, he did it more quickly. Like he couldn't bear to have anything touching his skin.

"They don't say Team Awesomest, do they?" Storm was asking Frost.

I looked over to see Frost pulling off his own socks and grinning at the fullback.

"Not yet," Frost said. "I'm still working on it." He grinned and wiggled his eyebrows playfully.

Storm shook his head and started to strip his own clothes off.

I didn't think Frost was working on it at all, but he couldn't resist stirring Storm up every chance he got. Could I blame him? Hell no, it was too easy to get under Storm's skin. I didn't hate the guy the way I used to, but I'd never stop stirring him up either. It was too much fun.

"You're getting along," Jay remarked. "With them."

I looked over to see him nod toward Storm and Frost.

"I never had a problem with Frosty," I said. Was that what had him on edge right now? Frost and whatever it was between him and I?

"I wasn't talking about Frosty," Jay said. "But you know that."

I grinned. "Sorry, couldn't help myself. Yeah, Storm might be okay. Sort of. Does that bother you?" My smile faded and I looked right at him, trying to figure out what was going through his brain. He was easier to read than some, but not at times like this. Not when he clearly had something on his mind and was still trying to work through it himself.

"That you two don't want to kill each other anymore?" Jay cocked his head at me. "I don't know, but it seems like a good thing to me. We're all on the same side here."

I was used to him not meeting my eyes, but he was more evasive than usual.

"Are you sure this isn't about Frost?" I asked, keeping my voice down low. Not that anyone would hear over the noise in the locker room.

We'd talked about the other guy before and I assured Jay I wasn't going to leave him for Frost. Jay and I were tight, that wasn't going to change as far as I was concerned.

"When you were down finding Dallas, Frost and I fucked Chelsea," he said.

I nodded slowly. "Okay. I'm all right with that." Was I? We weren't exclusive and never had been. Ever since we knew each other, there'd been other lovers. It was no big deal. It didn't change what we were to each other.

"I like her," he said slowly. "And I like him. And you like him."

"And I like her," I added. "Are you saying you want to be with him too?"

Jay's face was already pink from exertion, but it became darker now. "I don't want to mess things up between us. I know how I felt when Frost kissed you. I wanted to—" He held up his hands to mime strangling someone.

"Do you still feel that way?" I asked carefully. I thought I knew where he was going with this, but I didn't want to get too far ahead of the conversation.

"No," he said. "I want you to want whoever you want to want." He frowned at his own words. "You know what I mean."

I grinned. "Yeah. I think I got that."

He elbowed me in the side. "Don't be a fucker. I mean, if you want Chelsea and Frost, I'm okay with it. As long as you want me too."

"Of course I do." If we were anywhere but here, I would have kissed him. Once, I would have worried about getting hell from Storm about it. He wasn't a problem now, but there were other guys in the team who were less than enlightened. Not to mention the media who lingered around, wanting to report our win to whatever channel they worked for.

I didn't care what they had to say, but I didn't want them to be up in Jay's face. He didn't handle publicity as well as some of us. He found it over-whelming. It was better to keep him away from it, and it away from him.

"I want you, Chelsea and Frost," he admitted.

"All at once?" I raised a teasing eyebrow at him.

He gaped for a moment, then swallowed, his eyes shifting back and forth. "Yes?"

"Then that's what we'll do." I clapped him on the shoulder. I didn't think Chelsea or Frost would have a problem with that. In fact, I knew they wouldn't. They'd both be as into it as we would.

"You're the best." He offered me an awkward fist bump.

I wanted to hug him, but I bumped his fist and patted his bicep. "Let's hit the showers before everyone else does." And before standing here naked with him got too much and I bent him over one of the benches and fucked him boneless. He was having the same problem too, his cock half erect, pointing at me.

"Yeah," he said with the same regret.

I was tempted to kiss him anyway, because why should we hold back just because of what other people thought? I didn't, because the whole media thing was still relevant and important. I wanted to put him in lots of positions, but not where he was scrutinised until it became too much and he had a meltdown.

I'd seen that happen a couple of times before and he always hated himself afterwards, no matter how understanding or gentle I tried to be. He didn't like being unable to control and contain his emotions. No, it was much easier to prevent the problem before it became one.

As much as it frustrated him, this was one of the things I loved about him the most. Playing professional football was stressful, and avoiding the limelight was almost impossible. But he faced each day head on, even when it got too much. He was the bravest guy I knew. Men like Storm, who were big, confident and dominant, weren't as brave as Jay. Being arrogant was a lot easier than what he dealt with.

"I have an appointment with the real estate agent in the morning," I told him. "To see an apartment in Powell Tower. Want to come?"

We decided to share a house when we moved to Dusk Bay, but we occupied separate bedrooms. Never quite able to commit to more. I wasn't sure if he'd even want to move with me again.

"I wouldn't miss it," he said. "Do I get to pick my room?"

"If you like," I said with half a shrug.

"Can I pick the same room as you?" he asked carefully.

"I'd like it if you would," I said. "And Chelsea can have sleepovers with us." At least until we all gave in to Frost's desire to live in one big house together. We weren't quite there yet.

Jay grinned. "And Frost."

I glanced over to where Frost was chatting to Dallas about something. Dallas looked better than he had when we found him in the change area. When I first saw him, I thought he was dead. He looked like hell. Lucky for all of us, he was okay. Still shaken, but alive. He and Ramsey seemed to have struck up a friendship too, which I was totally here for.

"And Frost," I agreed.

Chapter Thirteen

Chelsea

"Nice place."

The apartment's layout was the same as Storm's, but this one was decorated with a butt ton of white. The countertops were white with light veining. The cabinets were white. The walls were painted off-white. Only the mid-tone hardwood broke it up.

"It could use some colour," Jay remarked. "Maybe a bright orange couch over there." He pointed.

"We're not having a bright orange couch," Atlas said.

Jay grinned. "Bright yellow?"

Atlas snorted. "Over my dead body."

Storm, who'd followed me into the apartment, opened his mouth.

Frost elbowed him in the ribs.

Storm turned to him. "What?"

"You were about to say that could be arranged," Frost said.

"I was not," Storm protested weakly. "I was going to say...something else."

"Like what?" Frost asked brightly. He was obviously trying to get a rise out of the fullback.

"He was going to say he agrees with me, right, Stormy?" Atlas asked, sliding him a sly grin.

"No, but I do," Storm said. "No way I'd have a bright yellow couch either." He looked mildly disgusted at the idea.

"What if I wanted one?" I asked.

He gave me a dark look. "Don't you start. Or do. Then I can take you upstairs for some punishment. It's been too long since I smacked your ass."

The real estate agent standing by the door raised his eyebrows at that, but turned away, pretending he hadn't heard.

"Let's have a look around here first," I said. I grabbed Storm's hand and pulled him towards the main bathroom. It was also a study in white on white.

"This could use some coloured tiles," Jay said.

"If you're about to suggest orange or yellow—" Atlas started.

Jay grinned.

"It might be that more than one ass that gets spanked," Frost said wistfully.

"Are you hoping yours is one of them?" I asked.

He grinned. "Always."

"If you don't stop that, I'm going to fuck one of you right here," Storm growled.

Frost and I exchanged glances.

"He said that like we'd mind," I remarked.

Storm's hand shot out to grab the back of Frost's head. "On your knees," he ordered. He pushed him down. "You too," he snapped at me and Jay.

Without bothering to look and make sure the real estate agent couldn't see, I lowered myself to my knees beside Frost.

The front of Storm's pants was already tented, seams straining. "Take my cock out," he said, teeth gritted.

Eyes on his, Frost pulled down the front of Storm's pants and boxers to free his erection. Thick and hard, his cock bobbed right in front of Frost's face, a bead of pre-cum already glistening on his tip.

"Open your mouth," he ordered. When Frost parted his lips, he pushed his cock all the way inside, to the back of his throat.

Atlas muttered something about going to make

an offer before he stepped out of the large bathroom and closed the door behind him, leaving the four of us in there.

"Are you okay with this?" I asked Jay. His gaze seemed to be half on Storm and half on the door Atlas just disappeared through. "You don't have to stay if you don't want to." I glanced defiantly at Storm, daring him to disagree.

"You can go if you want," Storm told him. His eyes were crossing as Frost sucked.

The wet sound of his mouth sent a spike of heat all the way through me. My clit pulsed with need. Knowing the real estate agent was still in the apartment got me going even more. My pussy was drenched already.

"I want to stay," Jay said after a few moments thought. His cock strained the front of his pants.

"Of course you do," Storm said approvingly. "Put that mouth to good use and make Chelsea come."

Neither of us needed to be told twice. I lay back on the cool tiles and let Jay push up my skirt and grab my panties. Making it look effortless, he tore them in two before stuffing both halves into his pocket. He murmured something about 'souvenir' before parting my thighs with his hands and lowering his face between them.

"That's it, make my woman feel good," Storm said. It was his turn to give me a challenging look. As if I might argue that I wasn't his woman. Or that I belonged to all of them.

With the way Jay expertly licked and sucked my clit, sliding his tongue inside me, I was in no mood to argue. Not to mention that coherent thought was quickly becoming difficult to come by.

Storm nodded his satisfaction and half closed his eyes to fuck Frost's mouth, his breathing becoming rapidly more ragged.

I grabbed Frost's hand and held onto him while he sucked, his other hand caressing Storm's balls. I squeezed it harder when I came against Jay's mouth, my back arching off the bathroom floor. I bit my lip hard, but lost the battle to keep myself from crying out loudly. My orgasm was so intense I lost all control, lost in a wave of bliss.

Storm was close behind, thrusting frantically before coming in Frost's mouth. "Don't swallow," he insisted. "I want you to share with Chelsea."

Smiling, Frost slid his mouth off Storm's cock and moved over to me. When I parted my lips, he let Storm's cum trickle from his mouth to mine.

Jay was watching with wide eyes, his shoulders still between my legs.

I raised an eyebrow at him before pushing myself up until I was sitting, and pressing my lips to Jay's salty ones. I tasted myself on him before I let him taste Storm, trickling the fullback's release into his eager mouth.

Jay slowly nodded his appreciation.

"Swallow it," Storm ordered.

"I have a better idea." Frost scooted over to Jay and slanted his mouth over the other man's. "Let me swallow it."

Jay tilted his face down, filling Frost's mouth while kissing him hard and deep. Their hands fumbled with the front of each other's pants before curling their fists around each other's cocks and pumping slowly.

"Did I say you could touch each other?" Storm tucked his own cock back into his pants.

"No, but if you tell me to stop now, I don't think I can," Frost said. "He feels so fucking good."

"So do you," Jay told him. Both men exchanged a heated glance before they resumed kissing, so frantic they all but devoured each other.

Storm grunted, but leaned back against the wall, his arms crossed, watching them both with dark eyes. His gaze flicked to me. "You like what you see?"

"I love what I see," I said.

Not just them touching, but the fact they seemed into each other. I hope that bond would grow over time, making our little family an even tighter knit. The only thing missing right now were Dallas and Ramsey, who were upstairs in Storm's apartment.

Ramsey said something about an important phone call and Dallas was tired after fucking me all night. More than once, I'd woken up just before he came. Only to go back to sleep with him nestled up to me. It was little wonder he was exhausted.

"Do you want to see them come?" Storm asked, his gaze back on the other two men.

"I want that very much," I said. Both Frost and Jay seemed very much there for it, or I would have responded differently. I'd never ask anything of them that they didn't want for themselves.

"You heard the woman," Storm said. "Show her how you come with each other."

Frost and Jay stroked each other faster now, more deliberate. They weren't just toying around with each other. While their lips and tongues tangled, they drew each other closer and closer to orgasms.

I couldn't tell who it was that grunted first, but then they were coming in each other's hands, squirting their release from their engorged heads, strings of cum decorating each other's hips. They continued to mash their mouths together for another couple of minutes before they managed to break apart and start to catch their breath.

Both of their mouths were red, lips swollen.

Frost smiled, satisfied.

Jay looked slightly more reserved, like always. Not unhappy, just with his emotions contained.

"You're good at that," Frost told him. "Any time you're down to do that again, so am I." He tucked Jay's cocked back into his pants and put them back into place, before doing the same to his own.

"Me too," Jay said awkwardly. "We should—" He started to rise to his feet when the bathroom door opened.

Atlas stepped back inside and glanced around to all of us with curiosity, but no judgement. "Looks like I missed all the fun."

"You were the one who left at the wrong time," Storm told him.

Atlas shrugged. "Someone had to finish the tour of the place. If anyone is interested, I made an offer. The agent seems to think it'll be accepted."

Frost stood and helped me to my feet. "Of course it will. Only a crazy person would turn down an offer from you."

"You said it," Atlas said.

Storm grunted a laugh. For once, he didn't try to contradict either of them out loud. His thoughts still showed in his expression. The smirk and the eye roll towards the ceiling said more than words ever could.

"This is a nice place." I hooked my arm through Atlas' and walked with him out of the bathroom.

"It is," he agreed. "Just what I was looking for, even without a yellow couch."

I didn't miss the stares and deep swallow from the real estate agent as we walked past him and out of the apartment. I knew he'd be discreet, he was too well-paid to be otherwise, but I suspected from the tent in the front of his pants, we might not be the only ones coming in the apartment today.

I hoped he enjoyed the entertainment.

Chapter Fourteen

Chelsea

"So, you'll be moving in downstairs." I nestled in closer to Atlas and spoke softly, so I didn't annoy the guys who were immersed in some action movie. It wasn't too hard to follow the plot without paying too much attention. Car chase, explosion, car chase. Nothing that required thought.

He squeezed me a little tighter. "Yeah, you good with that?"

"Let me think about that for a moment," I replied. "Having all of you closer to me all the time? Sounds perfect to me. Far enough away that you and Storm won't get on each other's nerves too much."

"He'll learn to like me eventually," Atlas said. "Ramsey is taking the spare room. We'll all be in the same building."

"Powell Tower will never be the same," I said with a laugh.

"I hope the place knows what it's in for." He chuckled. "So much awesomeness under one roof."

"However will the world cope?" I joked. "Seriously though, it'll be nice having everyone close by."

"Easier to keep tabs on everyone," he agreed. "And if anything happens, we'll all be there to deal with it."

It seemed more like a 'when' than an 'if,' but I decided not to bring that up. It wasn't as though we didn't both understand. I decided to broach another subject instead.

"Frost and Jay seem to be getting along well." They both sat together on the other couch, almost close enough to touch. Storm was on the other side of Frost, his attention on the huge screen.

"Yeah, they are." He glanced over to them, his expression softening.

"How do you feel about that?" I asked.

It took a moment for him to respond with, "I'm here for it. If they want to explore things between them, that's cool with me."

"And what about your feelings for both of them?" I asked gently. I was well aware the guys struggled to talk about their emotions at times. Especially when those feelings were new.

Atlas turned back to me, brown-gold eyes intense. "I love you," he said. "I love you and I love Jay. I could learn to love Frost too."

My heart melted a little more. "I love you too." I leaned over to press my lips to his. He tasted of coffee, with a hint of salt.

After a few moments, I pulled back and said, "I see why you'd feel that way about both of them too. Frost is sweet and I can totally see myself falling for Jay."

Truthfully, I already had. I was head over heels for all six of them. But things between Jay, Ramsey and I were still growing and I wanted to nurture them, not rush in headlong. In theory, we had plenty of time for that.

"Jay is someone special," Atlas whispered. "Sometimes I think I don't deserve him. I'm not sure I deserve you either, to be frank. Storm isn't wrong when he calls me an asshole. I'm not wrong when I call him one," he added quickly, half-laughing.

I shoved my elbow into him. "You're not an asshole and neither is he. If you didn't deserve me, I wouldn't be here with you right now. I'm very particular about who I spend time with. And who I fuck."

His body stiffened slightly. He looked like he wanted to ask something, but wasn't sure if he should.

"What is it?" I asked. I gave him my best 'out with it' face.

"When you used to work at Flirts," he started tentatively.

"Was I particular about who I fucked?" I asked. "Not really. As long as they paid and didn't want me to do something I didn't want to."

"What was that like?" he asked.

"You've never fucked a stranger?" I asked. He travelled all over the world, playing rugby. He would have had all sorts of people throwing themselves at him. I very much doubted he said no to all of them, or even any of them.

His mouth opened and closed a couple of times before he conceded, "Yeah, a few times. More than a few, I guess."

"It's no different, except I got paid," I said. "It was just sex. You wouldn't think twice about who you tackle, would you?"

"No," he agreed. He glanced away for a couple of moments, then back again. "Did you switch off when it happened? Think about other things?" He gave the impression he was asking for a particular reason.

"Sometimes," I admitted. "But I've never done that with any of you. When we fuck, I'm one hundred percent present. Enjoying every moment of it."

From the relief in his eyes, I'd answered the question he hadn't asked yet. Was I on autopilot when I had sex, after having done it with so many men I'd lost count a long time ago? I understood why he'd think that, but it was never that way with any of the guys. That was fucking, this was making love.

"Thank you," he whispered. "I enjoy every moment with you too. It's different from before. It... means something." He shifted uncomfortably the closer he got to talking about anything too emotional.

"It means everything," I said. "You six are it for me. There'll never be anyone else."

"There'll never be anyone but you, Jay and potentially Frost," he replied.

"So, you won't be getting together with Storm?" I asked teasingly.

He snorted. "Not like that, no. I think we're too alike. We'd kill each other."

"We definitely don't want that," I said with mock-alarm. The fact they were sitting together in the same room and not slinging insults back and forth was enough for now. Hopefully someday they'd actually like each other, but having called a truce, that was a good start.

"Definitely not," he agreed. He kissed me again, his hand sliding down my side and over my belly. "I'll tell you what I want though."

"Yeah, what's that?" I asked.

He responded with a husky laugh. "You. I want you." He tugged up the hem of my shirt and slipped his hand underneath. He kissed my mouth, his tongue sliding over my lips while his thumb traced circles around my bare skin, all the way up to my breasts.

"No bra, I like it." He ran the pad of his thumb over my nipple until it was a hard peak and I was moaning, ready for more.

"You know what would be even better?" he asked. "If you never wear clothes again. You could walk around here naked all day long in nothing but a pair of heels."

"Mmm, I like the sound of that," I said breathlessly. "I will if you will."

"I'll be naked with you any time." He lowered his mouth to my nipple and sucked slowly, swirling his tongue around my sensitive skin and teasing with his teeth. He moved over to give the other nipple the same attention before sliding his hand down the front of my track pants. Technically, they were Frost's track pants, but I borrowed them. I was sure he wouldn't mind.

"No panties," he said approvingly. He undid the tie at the front of the pants and pushed them down until they slid off my ankles.

I sat up just enough to pull my shirt off the rest of the way before nestling against him again, completely bare.

"Much better," he said. "I think I might go and burn all of your clothes, so you stay like this forever."

"I might raise some eyebrows at work," I said.

"No leaving the apartment," he said. "Let's stay here forever and fuck." He gripped my wrist and pushed down the front of his pants until I wrapped my fingers around his cock.

"That sounds nice." I worked his cock for a couple of minutes, slowly, languidly, before freeing it from his pants and swinging my leg over his hips. Facing him, I lowered myself down onto his erection, watching his eyes half close with bliss.

He cupped my breasts and palmed my nipples while I rose and fell in his lap, riding his cock.

I was so engrossed in the expression on his face, I didn't see Dallas beside us until he was taking my chin in his hand and turning my face so he could slide his cock between my lips.

"Fuck, yeah," Atlas whispered. "You're incredible." He turned and lay back along the couch, careful not to dislodge my pussy or Dallas' cock.

"She really is," Dallas breathed. He fucked my mouth like we hadn't fucked in a year. Eager and hard.

"She can take more," Storm said. He held a tube of lube in his hand. "Lean forward," he said to me.

When I leaned as far forward as I could, he squeezed lube onto his fingers and smeared a generous portion on my rear hole. Slowly, he eased one finger inside, then another. Stretching me and making me ready.

Finally, he straddled Atlas' legs and pressed the tip of his cock into my tight hole.

I moaned with the pressure that felt so good I thought I might explode. Pleasure that got better when he pushed in deeper, until he was all the way inside me.

"Remind her we own her," he said to Atlas and Dallas. "Show her who she belongs to."

"You admit we own her too?" Atlas asked teasingly.

"Fuck her before I have Frost, Ramsey or Jay take your place," Storm snapped. "They'd be happy to."

Atlas glanced off to the side. "Jay and Frost seem a bit busy right now."

I couldn't see past Dallas, but I was picturing them kissing and touching each other. Enjoying each other the way I enjoyed having three of my guys inside me.

I pressed the flat of my palms against Atlas' chest as Storm thrust into me from behind with slow, deliberate strokes. At the same time, I rolled my hips and sucked, adding to the friction of Atlas' and Dallas' thrusts. Each one was in perfect rhythm with Storm's.

Storm increased the speed, forcing the other two to do the same. Or maybe it was something instinctual. Either way, they filled me at the same pace while I quickly edged towards oblivion.

My first orgasm hit with the force of a tsunami, and the second half a minute later. I gasped, panted and moaned around Dallas' cock, but didn't stop sucking and licking. Didn't stop rolling my hips to draw out my own pleasure as well as Atlas'. My cry was muffled, but not silenced.

Dallas followed, thrusting frantically before

coming in the back of my throat, squirting sweet cum into my mouth. I swallowed before he even slid his cock out from between my lips.

Panting, he stepped away, giving me a view of Frost and Jay. Frost was on his knees, his mouth around Jay's cock. His hand massaging the other player's balls. The sight made me come for a third time, harder and faster than before.

In turn, I stole orgasms from both Storm and Atlas, each coming deep inside me at the same time, with matching grunts and groans of bliss.

We all sagged, panting for breath before Storm slid out of me carefully and slapped my ass.

"My turn," Ramsey said. He was already naked as he offered me his hand and helped me off Atlas. He led me over to the rug on the floor in front of the window.

Then Dallas was beside me, helping me down again and pulling me on top of him before lowering me onto his cock, which was already hard again. I leaned forward and let Ramsey grip my hips before pushing himself into my rear hole.

"Frost," Storm said. "Get over here and fuck her mouth."

Frost, who was licking his lips, crouched down

beside me and did what Storm told him to. "Just so you know, Jay's cum is really tasty."

I smiled around my mouthful and sucked while all three of them thrust inside me, filling me again. This time was different to fucking on the couch with Atlas and Storm. Their cocks hit me differently, but just as good. I was slower to come this time, but it was just as intense and wonderful. Like before, Frost was the first to come, filling my mouth until I swallowed.

He was quickly followed by Ramsey, who grunted and moaned before coming in my ass.

Dallas was last, but only by a handful of moments. Thrusting up into me like he could never get enough of being inside me. Like all there was in the world was my pussy and his cock. He moaned loudly and fell still, exploding inside me for a second time before flopping back against the rug.

"Fuck," Frost whispered. "You are something else, woman."

"She's perfect," Storm said. "And she's ours." After a beat, he added, "Let's get her cleaned up."

That was a good idea, because with so much cum inside me, I'd make a mess if I sat back down on the couch. I wouldn't have it any other way.

There was nothing like being fucked by six incredible men to make me forget reality for a while.

Unwelcome, it crashed back into my mind along with questions.

What was India up to, and who was Nile Fox?

Chapter Fifteen

Chelsea

"She was quite the interesting person," Ice remarked. He leaned forward, propping his elbow on the table and took a sip of beer.

"Why is that?" Storm asked. He looked over the table at my brother, his eyes narrowed.

Hazards was relatively quiet for this time of night. My brother, Storm, Ramsey, Dallas and I sat around a table. Frost, Jay and Atlas were playing pool and laughing about something. As usual, Dallas sat as close to me as he could, his hand on my thigh.

"From what I can tell, India was popular with staff and customers," Ice said slowly, giving me a slight tilt of his head. "She did well at school. She got into university to study veterinary science, but never went."

"She went straight from school to working at Flirts," I said. "She never said anything about getting into uni. Mostly she talked about being close to her family and things like that." He was right though, everyone adored her.

"How does that make her interesting?" Storm asked. "Plenty of people don't go to university."

"That's true," Ice agreed. "But from the start she had more in her bank account than the average employee of Flirts. We've traced a bunch of payments that went in every month. Divina wasn't her only employer. She probably owed a ton in back taxes."

"Avoiding tax doesn't mean she deserved what... happened to her," Dallas said awkwardly.

"It depends where the money came from," I said. "Let me guess, Carlos Jones?"

"We haven't traced it directly to him, but that's pretty much the direction it's going, yes," Ice agreed. "An associate of mine suggested India had connections to a number of young people who went missing. A big enough number to warrant looking deeper into it."

"Missing—" Dallas stared at Ice. "You mean they were trafficked?"

"That would be my suspicion." Ice took another

sip of his beer. "If I had to guess, I'd say Carlos Jones paid her to bring him people."

I blinked at him a couple of times. "She seemed so nice. I can't believe she'd be involved in something like that."

"People say the same about me." He smiled. "And yet, here we are." He raised his hand out to the side. "Chelsea, did she ever approach you in a way that suggests she tried to coerce you into a dangerous position?"

"She better fucking not," Storm growled.

"She's already dead," I pointed out.

"Doesn't matter, I'd still..." He shook his head. "I don't know. Something that would make her glad she's already dead."

Dallas squeezed my thigh. "Did she do anything like that to you?"

I leaned into him and thought carefully. "Not that I can think of, specifically. She invited me to her place a couple of times, but either I had to work, or had to study. Or I was having dinner with Isaac, Mum and Dad."

Storm growled. "She might have done something to you if you'd gone."

The thought made my blood run cold. "I guess

it's possible. She wouldn't have gotten very far with me."

"Absolutely not," my brother agreed. "No one kidnaps my sister and gets away with it. Unless she consents." He gave me a sly smile.

Dallas let out a ragged breath, clearly remembering when he, Storm and Frost bundled me into the back of the car and took me to Frost's cabin. I didn't need to look, to know he was hard now. His expression was already strained.

"If India tried to have Chelsea taken, we might have found out what she was up to sooner," Ice said with a rare hint of regret. "We would have got to her before anything happened and figured it all out."

"You seem very sure about that," Storm said. "That you'd get to Chelsea before anyone laid a hand on her."

"If they tried, Chelsea would have given them hell," Ice told him. "She looks sweet, but she has a mean right hook. Between growing up with me and studying at Brutham Academy, she's learned how to take care of herself."

"Not to mention working at Flirts," I said. "You had to know how to handle people, or they'd take advantage."

I tried to look confident, but he seemed to have

more faith in me than I had in myself. If I was held at gunpoint, or drugged, I'd be hard pressed to fight back. If they roofied me like Frost did, I couldn't stop them from raping me. The idea was terrifying.

"You definitely know how to handle people," Dallas said softly. He lightly pressed his head to mine, inhaling my scent and burying his face in my hair. "You know how to handle me."

"You're easy to handle, because you'd never do anything to hurt me," I whispered. "Except in the way I like to be hurt."

"You've done a good job handling Atlas too," Storm said. "He's almost not a complete asshole anymore."

"He'd say the same about you," Ramsey said. He'd sat quietly, listening to the conversation and looking thoughtful, if pissed off at the suggestion India might have tried to have me trafficked.

"Probably," Storm agreed. "He'd be wrong though. I'm still an asshole. And I'm okay with that. Someone has to be, to keep the rest of you in line. For Chelsea's sake."

"You like being in control," Ramsey observed. "Chelsea's sake or not."

Storm shrugged. "Maybe I do. You know what

I'm not going to do? Apologise for it. It's who I am, and I'm not going to change for anyone."

"We wouldn't ask you to." I leaned over and put a hand on his. "It's one of things we like about you. You don't hold back. You say what you're thinking and everyone knows where they stand with you. It's a refreshing change from trying to figure out what's going on inside people's heads."

"There's only one thing going on inside my head," Dallas said. He moved his hand up my thigh, and between my legs.

"You don't want to see inside mine," Ramsey said.

I shifted my gaze over to him. "You think I'd be scared of what I saw in there?"

"You should be. I am." He took a sip of his own light beer and shrugged a shoulder.

"That sounds like a challenge to me," I said. "I don't think someone who would take me on a hot air balloon ride to watch the sunrise could really be that bad."

"That might be what he wants you to think." Storm squinted at Ramsey, as if trying to figure him out. "Lull you into a false sense of security before he... I don't know what. Are you sure you're not working with Carlos Jones?"

"Not a chance," Ramsey said. "I wouldn't work with a trafficker."

"That's good, because any hint that you planned to traffic Chelsea and I'll be the next person on the team to kill someone," Storm growled.

"Don't threaten me," Ramsey said without flinching. "I could end you before you move." He could have out glared Storm with the look he was giving him now.

"You guys are kinda hot," Ice remarked. "No wonder Chelsea is into you."

They both turned to look at him until he grinned with no hint of apology. "What? I'm very taken, but I can admire hot people when I meet them."

"Of course you can," I told him. "They're both very hot." It was probably just as well my brother was taken, because I suspected he would have found a way into our little family of seven. I could see him sharing Frost and Jay with me. Maybe Atlas too. We'd always been close, but that would have been one hell of a tangle.

"Dallas is too," I said before he felt left out.

"Dallas is hot for you," Dallas said. "Always."

"I'm hot for you too," I told him. I took a moment to clear my head and get the conversation back on track. "Isaac, is there any way of tracking the people

India trafficked? Could we find them and return them to their families?"

He raised an eyebrow and cocked his head. "Look at you, wanting to take on the big bad. People like him tend to keep a tight leash on anyone they steal. Once they disappear into that world, it can be difficult to get them back."

"But not impossible," I stated. "I know it's happened before."

When Storm and Dallas glanced at me, I said, "One of the Bell sisters was trafficked. Back when the Bell family was the main rival of the Brantley family. She got free and freed all the women with her." Only a brave or stupid person would do that to one of those women. They were powerful and had powerful friends.

"Most people aren't the Bell sisters," Ice pointed out. "Had she disappeared into the network, she might not have been found again."

"Are you saying we can't find them, so we shouldn't try?" Storm asked.

"He saying it's dangerous," Ramsey said.

"Exactly," Ice agreed. "They might not be alive anymore. But now we know India was involved, we can look at who she was working with. Maybe we can uncover something. I won't make any promises except that I'll try."

That was all I was going to get, so I nodded. "Thank you. I don't want to take on any big bad anything, but their families should know what happened to them."

"I agree, totally," Ice said. "I've never been a fan of trafficking. The Brantley family does less of it these days than they used to, thanks to the twins. The only one involved nowadays is Caleb. In his case, it's probably to piss Hunter and Parker off."

"Who's Caleb?" Dallas asked.

"Reuben Brantley's younger brother," I said. "Second in command of the family business. Older brother of Hunter and Parker. If anyone is getting their hands dirty these days, it's usually him."

"Total narcissist without any remorse," Ice said. "If the man has a soft spot for anything, I've never seen it. And you know me, I like to see the soft spot in anyone."

"Sounds like a total prince," Storm said sarcastically.

"He's an asshole," Ramsey said. "Still better than Carlos Jones."

"This Jones guy must be a real prick then," Storm said.

"Total prick," Ramsey agreed. "Prick that is going to be annoyed we killed one of his contacts."

I sighed softly and leaned over towards my brother to ask, "Do you have any idea who Nile Fox is?"

Ice cocked his head in thought. "I can't say I do. Why?"

"India said something about him before I...she died," Dallas said. "He's got something to do with Otis Skinner and Dominic King."

"Huh." Ice scratched the side of his head. "It doesn't ring a bell. She didn't say anything more about him?"

"Not that I remember," Dallas said. His brow creased in thought. "She thought I should know who he is. When I didn't, she came at me."

"Interesting," Ice said. "I haven't got a clue, sorry. I'll ask around and see what I can find. If he's that high profile, he shouldn't be too hard to track down. He might be operating under some sort of codename, and only a select few know his real name."

I nodded slowly. "That's possible. I'm sure you'll figure out who he is, if we don't find out first."

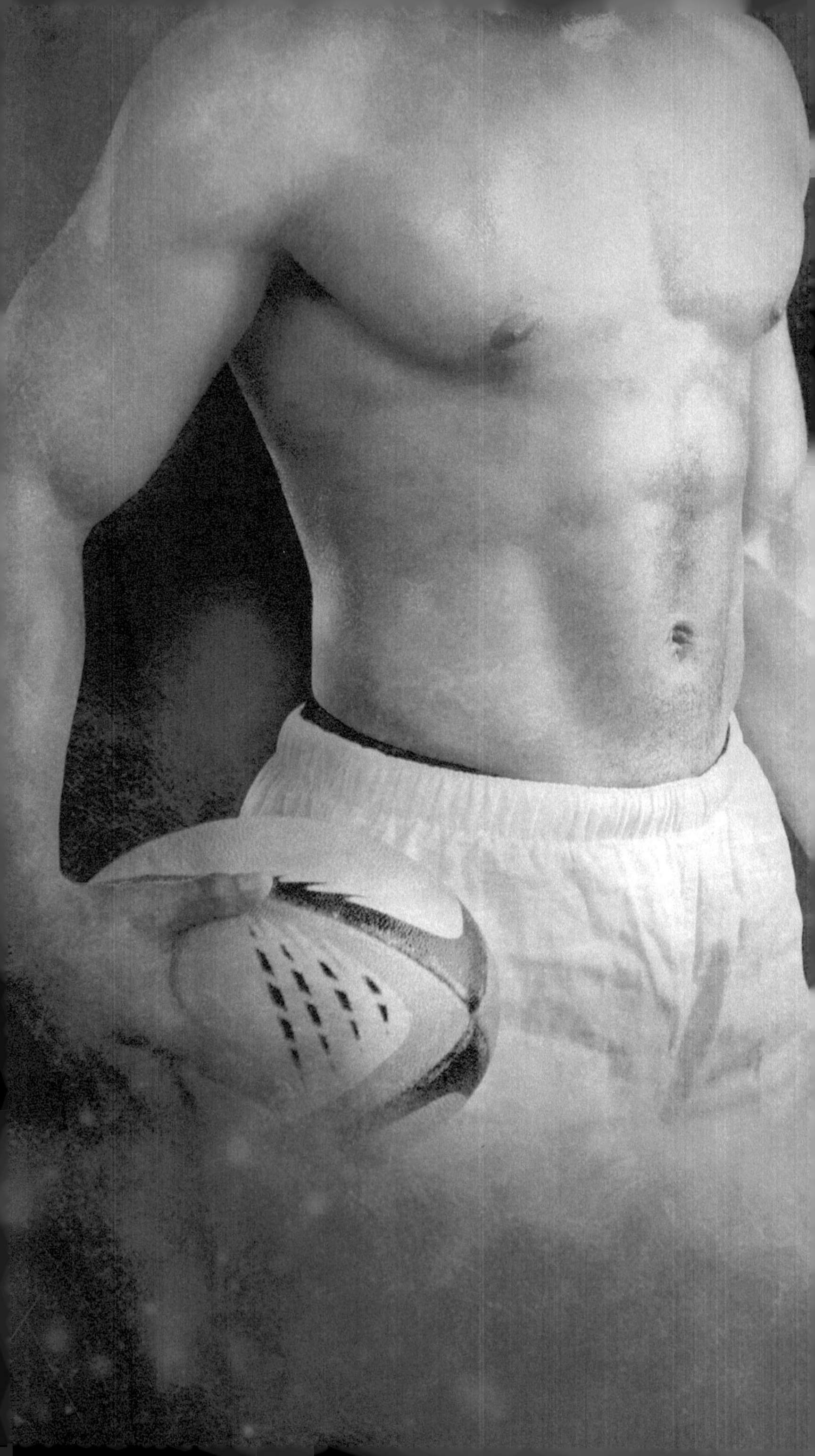

Chapter Sixteen

Chelsea

Dallas held my hand as we walked along the street toward Powell Tower. The night was cool. A steady flow of traffic passed us by.

The other guys walked behind us, Storm and Frost talking about training and next Friday night's game.

"Can I tell you something?" Dallas asked.

"Of course you can," I said. "Anything." He looked pensive, but I wasn't worried. There was nothing he could say that would bother me, or that I wouldn't support. Nothing I could think of, anyway.

"I don't feel bad about what I did to her," he admitted. "India, I mean. If she was involved in what your brother said she was involved in, then she kind of, I dunno, deserved it. Especially if she would have done that to you. Traffic you." He shuddered. "Is that wrong? I shouldn't feel good about what I did."

"I don't think it's wrong at all," I said. "I feel bad for not seeing who she was. Maybe I could have prevented her from doing what she was doing."

How many people had she trafficked without me having a clue? I couldn't help feeling responsible for whatever happened to them while I was oblivious. How many lives had she ruined while I got on with mine? I couldn't bring myself to be sad she was dead either. People like her brought misery to other people. She wouldn't have been out of place chained in my brother's workroom. He would have had fun with someone like her. Teaching her to suffer the way her victims suffered, and might still be suffering.

"Don't feel bad," he told me. "I met her, she seemed nice. I wouldn't have expected her to do what she did either. I guess that's why she got away with it. It's easy to suspect bad people of being bad, not nice ones."

"Maybe I was too trusting," I said. It wasn't usually like me to take people at face value, but with her, I had. And people suffered because of it.

"It's tiring being suspicious of everyone," he said. "Besides, you had a lot going on in your life. Work and study. No one expects you to pick up on everything all the time."

"I grew up here. I should have better developed instincts for things like that. Especially when she was right there, in front of my face." I sighed softly, my breath misting the air in front of me.

I expected it of myself, but the more I thought about it, the more that didn't make sense. He was right, I couldn't be tuned in to everything all the time. I was exhausted so often from being so busy, I probably missed a million cues before lunchtime.

Okay, nowhere near that, but I should have been more aware. I would be more aware from now on.

"She's not in front of your face anymore," he said. "She won't be able to do that to anyone else." He sounded almost proud of himself now.

"Because of you." I squeezed his hand. "Because you stayed to listen to her. Because your gut told you she couldn't be trusted, and you listened to it."

Why did mine let me down so badly? Was there anyone else I shouldn't trust that I hadn't picked up on yet?

For about half a second, I thought of the guys, but immediately dismissed it. I knew I could trust them. There was no doubt in my mind. Obviously, I could trust my brother, and his partners. I could trust Divina and Sadie.

Apart from them, there was no one else. I liked Daisy Lasalle, but trust her? Not completely. Not when she was happy to drag me back into this crazy lifestyle. I sure as hell wouldn't trust anyone with the last name Brantley. Caleb Brantley might be the worst, but I wouldn't turn my back on any of them. I was just as likely to find a knife between my ribs if I did.

"Yeah," he said softly. "Something about her was off."

"She was just about to cash in on a big payday and walk away from Flirts," I said. "She got sloppy. She got confident and it got her killed. If she played it cool, like she always had with me, she might not have given you an excuse to kill her."

What was she thinking, lunging at him? Even if she was skilled and took him by surprise, he was so much bigger than her. Fit, strong and athletic. With a ruthless streak he displayed on the field all the time.

"And she'd still be doing what she was doing." He grimaced. "I'm glad she got cocky."

He huffed out a breath. "I can still feel her blood on my hand. It was so warm and...sticky. The smell of it is still in my nose. Her scream... The sounds she made when she died. Everything after that is a blur, but those are crystal-clear in my brain. I keep playing them over and over in my head. They won't stop replaying. Sometimes it's in slow motion, moment by moment, like time slowed down. Sometimes it's a flash of everything that happened in a heartbeat. Sometimes I dream about it and it feels more real than reality."

"That sounds confronting," I said softly.

"It is," he said. "But I don't hate what I did. I... I don't think I'd hate what I did if she was innocent." The last came out as a whisper.

"You liked killing her?" I asked. I didn't see a need to dance around the question. He wanted to talk about it, so I'd be direct, giving him the chance to do the same.

"I felt powerful," he said. "I felt...like it was over too fast. When it rushes through my mind, I try to slow it down and live it again and again. The look in her eyes as her life faded away. I never want to forget that. I *know*, that's fucked up."

"She wasn't innocent," I reminded him. I didn't want him to torment himself for enjoying what he did. He wasn't the first person I knew who enjoyed killing. He probably wouldn't be the last. Him, my brother and Frost were in good company, especially in Dusk Bay.

"No, but what if next time it is an innocent person?" he asked. His voice wavered.

"You're not the sort of person who is going to kill indiscriminately," I said. "She came at you and you reacted. An innocent person isn't going to do that." At least, I hoped they wouldn't. "What were you supposed to do anyway? Let her kill you?"

"No, but, what if I lose control?" he asked. "You know there's times I have to fuck you or I'll lose my mind. All I can think of is being inside you. It's like the whole world disappears and the only thing that matters is your pussy. Or your mouth. What if that happens, but instead of fucking, I need to kill?"

"Are you worried you'll kill me?" I asked. Was that what this was about? I knew how he was when it came to fucking. He held nothing back, even if he'd only just come inside me. Every time he fucked me was like the first time. Always energetic, bordering on desperation. Addiction. I loved every moment of it. But if that turned into a need to kill, he'd be dangerous as hell.

He stopped and turned to me, horrified. "I would never do that. I'd throw myself off the top of Powell Tower before I hurt you."

"But you're worried about it anyway," I said. "That you'll do it without thinking, then realise what you've done."

He hung his head. "I'm scared," he whispered. "I can't lose it around you. Not like that. Right now, all I want to do is push you up against the wall and fuck you like hell, but what if it's more?"

I placed my hands on his cheeks and pulled his face down to mine. "That won't happen," I said firmly. "I know you better than that. You're not going to snap and kill me. Besides, like my brother said, I can take care of myself. And there's five other guys who'd stop you anyway." I jerked my head to where they'd all stood, watching us carefully.

He glanced over to them. "They'd kill me." Rather than looking scared at the idea, he seemed relieved. Content to know while they were around, there were lines he couldn't cross even if he completely lost his mind. They'd be there to hold him back if he couldn't do it himself. Like a safety net under a tightrope walker.

"Probably," I agreed. "But you won't give them a reason to. What happened with India, was one moment. If you want to feel that powerful again, I'm sure my brother can arrange for you and Frost to work with him. You can work through your rage with people who deserve it. You'll find a way to keep it contained. Okay?"

I looked him in the eyes, my gaze firm, waiting for a response. In the back of my mind, I was fully aware regular people didn't have conversations like this. Organising my brother to let my boyfriends kill people just for the fun of it. On the other hand, maybe it was more normal than I realised. In this city at least, it probably was.

"Okay," he whispered. "I want that. I don't want to hurt anyone who's innocent. Not you, not anyone." He shook his head slightly, but he was trembling again, pent-up emotions threatening to overflow.

"I know you don't," I said. "You're a good man, Dallas Gregory. Being a little bit morally grey doesn't change that. It doesn't change how I feel about you. I love you." I pressed my lips to his.

"I love you too." He kissed me back. "You really think I'm a good man? That morally grey bit sounds more accurate." His hazel eyes scanned back and forth, taking in my expression, uncertainty in his gaze.

"I think I speak for all of us when I say morally grey is awesome," Frost remarked.

"Fuck yeah it is," Atlas agreed. "Life is too short to be too much of a goody-goody."

"No one would ever accuse you of being a goody-goody," Storm told him. "Me either, come to think of it. Fuck that. I'd be bored out of my brain in about three seconds flat."

"Me too," Frost agreed.

"Same," Ramsey said.

"It's not so bad," Jay deadpanned.

We all turned to stare at him.

He shrugged, barely containing a smile. "Someone has to be the goody-goody around here. It's none of you, so why can't it be me?"

"Because we know you better than that," Atlas told him. "I do anyway. Love you bro, but you ain't a goody-goody. In fact, I think Team Morally Grey might be appropriate for all of us."

"I'll get onto ordering the jackets," Frost joked. "I know the T-shirt version exists. I've seen them on social media."

"Is it something you want to announce to the world?" I asked.

"Definitely," Frost agreed. "Morally grey and proud of it."

"I don't think the team would like that too much," I said.

He hesitated for a moment, then made a face. "You're right. They wouldn't. Killjoys. Fine, I'll keep my morally grey personality under wraps until I retire. After that, I make no promises."

"Don't worry." Storm wrapped an arm around his shoulders. "We know what you're like. You can be out, loud and proud around us."

Frost leaned against him and grinned. "You guys are the best."

"Hell yeah we are," Storm agreed.

"Let's go home," Dallas said. "If I don't fuck Chelsea soon, my balls are going to explode." He looked pained.

"We don't want that," I said. "That would be messy."

"Yeah." He took my hand and we resumed walking.

Chapter Seventeen

Chelsea

We barely made it through the door before Dallas pulled off my leggings and panties, pinning me to the wall and hooking a hand under my knee. He raised my leg and barely managed to get his cock out before he slammed it into me.

"I'm addicted to you," he said breathlessly. "If there's a support group, I don't care."

"We are the support group." Frost clapped him on the shoulder on the way past. "We support you fucking her whenever you need to."

"Amen," Storm agreed. He ushered the others past until Dallas roared out his orgasm in unison with mine. No sooner had Dallas pulled out of me than Storm took my hand and tugged me into the main bedroom. He scooped me up and tossed me onto the bed.

"Take the rest of your clothes off," he ordered. He stood with his hands on his hips, watching me while I hurried to comply.

"She can be very obedient," Ramsey remarked, coming to stand beside Storm.

"When she wants to be," Storm agreed. "What about you?"

"I'm not going to do what you tell me to do," Ramsey said evenly.

"Same here," Storm said. "I guess we'll both be telling her what to do."

"Works for me," Ramsey said. He raised his eyebrow at me. "Put your hands up above your head. Do you have something to tie her wrists together?"

Storm opened the drawer beside the bed and pulled out a length of shibari rope in bright red. He offered it to Ramsey.

"Perfect." Ramsey sat beside me, tying one end of the rope around my wrists and the other to the bed. "On your knees, hands on the headboard."

Enough slack remained that I could turn all the way around, my hands gripping the cool wood, ass in the air.

"I like her like this," Storm said. He shed his clothes and sat beside me to pinch my nipple hard.

I let out a squeak, but it was a combination of pleasure and pain. He smiled and pinched me again.

Ramsey pushed his hand between my legs and ran the side of his fingers across my pussy and back again. "She's wet from Dallas' cum and her release. Tell me, Chelsea, whose slut are you?" He ran his fingers back the other way.

"Yours," I said, quivering. "I'm your slut."

Ramsey slapped my ass. "That's right. Ours."

"It's taken her a while to admit we own her," Storm said. "I told her right from the start and she resisted. Now she gets it. She's our fuck toy. Our possession. We get to do whatever we want with her body."

If he kept talking like that, I was going to come right then and there.

"Fuck toy," Ramsey repeated slowly. "I like that." He pulled off his shirt and covered my eyes with it before tying the sleeves behind my head. "She won't know who's inside her."

Storm chuckled. "I like that. We can fuck her and she won't know whose cock is in her pussy." He pinched my nipple again before they moved around.

I quickly lost track of who was where. I thought I

heard another set of footsteps enter the room, but I had no idea who they belonged to.

Someone touched my ass, then a finger was pressed into my pussy, followed by another. Then a third. They were removed slowly, then rammed back in again.

Several times, they finger fucked me before pulling them out and replacing them with their cock.

Another one of them grabbed my face, turned it and pushed their cock between my lips. It wasn't Ramsey, because they didn't have any piercings. Apart from that, I couldn't tell. They tasted good, but I couldn't pin down the particular flavour. Did it matter? I decided it didn't. All that did was that one guy was fucking my pussy while another was fucking my mouth. Without being able to see, all I could do was enjoy the way it felt. Ragged breathing and moans all around me. Sweat and need.

Someone on the other side of me ran his hand down my chest and over my breasts, making my nipples harder. They didn't pinch, but once again I couldn't tell whose hands they were.

One hand moved from my breasts, down to my pussy, stroking my clit while whoever was behind me thrust. The excitement of not knowing pushed me quickly back to the edge.

Right now, I was exactly what they wanted me to be. Their fuck toy. My body was theirs to use, to ruin. To come deep inside.

Firm hands gripped my hips tight as they drove into me harder and harder before coming with a series of moans and grunts. Soft enough that I couldn't pick out who they belonged to. Then they were sliding out of me and I was rolled over onto my back before a different cock was pressed into me.

The cock I was sucking was pushed back into my mouth, all the way to my throat. Over and over they pushed in as far as they could go, making me gag each time. They held my head in place with a hand and relentlessly fucked my mouth, holding back nothing, using me as hard as they could.

It was perfect. I could have done this for hours.

A hot pair of hands grabbed my legs and raised them over their shoulders so they could pound deeper into me. So deep it hurt, but I could only cry out in pleasure, wanting more. Deeper, harder, everything.

The guy beside me gave a grunt and ground his cock in deeper still before coming right at the back of my throat. So deep I almost choked on his cum. I managed to swallow and gasp a couple of breaths before he slid out of me.

The man who was fucking my pussy followed a few moments later, coming hard and fast inside me, pulling me down into another orgasm of my own. Together we panted and gasped, grunted and moaned.

Nothing in the world existed in those moments except this and a million exploding stars. I shattered into countless pieces before gradually coming back together and flopping against the mattress.

I thought I was done when the wet cock was sliding out of my pussy and my legs were lowered to the bed, but then I was turned back onto my stomach and another was sliding into me from behind. I wanted to scream that I couldn't take any more. At the same time, I wanted to yell for them to keep going. Tears slid down my cheeks, but I didn't want them to stop. Not until they were totally finished with me. I wanted them fully satisfied, as boneless as I was going to be.

They were slower now, thrusting in and out of me as though they had all the time in the world. I supposed they did. We had nowhere else to be right now. Nowhere but here.

Gradually, he increased the speed, driving in harder with each stroke before he finally shuddered and came, his cock buried all the way inside me. Filling me with his hot cum.

He sagged over me, weight half on and half off my body.

"Fuck," he whispered.

I smiled. I knew that voice. Dallas, of course. He never could only go one round with me.

He managed to roll off me and undid Ramsey's shirt before pulling it off my eyes.

I turned around to face him. Ramsey and Storm sat on either side of the bed, watching us both.

"Are you going to untie me?" I asked.

"I like you like this," Storm said.

"Me too," Frost said, appearing in the doorway. Atlas and Jay were right behind him. "I vote we leave her like that."

"No," Dallas said. He started to untie the rope. "She needs a nice hot bath now."

"Good idea," Frost said. "Get her cleaned up for round two."

"There you go, threatening me with a good time again," I teased as Dallas scooped me up in his arms.

"It's not a threat." Frost followed us to the bathroom and turned on the tap to fill the bath with hot water. "It's a promise." He added some rose scented bath salts and threw in a bath bomb for good measure. When the water was high enough, he checked the temperature and nodded for Dallas to lower me in.

"Something you should know about me," Frost said. He leaned in until the tips of our noses were touching. "I always keep my promises."

"Me too," I said. I sank down deep into the water and let Frost wash my back. "I promise to let you enjoy my body when I'm nice and clean."

"Cute that she thinks she has a choice," Storm said.

I gave him a smile. I knew I always had a choice, but his dirty talk was one of my favourite things about him. That and being his usual growly, possessive self.

Chapter Eighteen

Chelsea

"How's your range of movement?" I looked critically at Ramsey's knee.

He placed his palm against the wall, bent and flexed his leg, then did the same with the other knee. "It's okay. Just a little stiff first thing in the morning."

"You've been doing the exercises Doctor Skinner and your PT set out for you?" I asked.

"And then some," he agreed. "Better to do too much than too little."

"Have you been overdoing it?" I cocked my head at him. When he wasn't training, he seemed to be in the gym or the pool at home.

He frowned, but it was a cagey look at best.

"I'll take that as a yes," I said. "There is such a thing as too much."

He pushed off the wall and crossed his arms defensively. "I like to work out."

"So do I," I said. "But if you do too much of it, you can cause damage to your body. Do you want to end your career because you're exercising too much?" I wasn't telling him anything he didn't already know. That was obvious by his body language. "I don't want to give you a lecture."

"Then don't," he said evenly. "I'm good."

"Are you?" I straightened my head. "In my experience, people who exercise too much do it for a reason. Do you want to talk about it?" I spoke as gently as I could, while still firm. At the end of the day, I was still his doctor. His health was a priority. Physical and mental.

He glanced down at the floor. "I like to work out," he said again.

"Okay, but why?" I asked. "Look, you don't have to talk about it to me if you don't want to, but there are other people you can talk to. A professional, or one of the guys. We'll help you get through this." Whatever "this" was.

"I'll think about it," he said evasively. "Don't be on my case."

"Don't forget it's my job to be on your case," I said

unapologetically. "As your doctor and as your girlfriend."

He looked up at me, his head tilted. "That what you are? My girlfriend?"

"I'd say so," I said, unflinching. "Unless you have a problem with that?"

"No problem," he said. "I like the sound of it."

"Me too." I turned to type in the details of his appointment into my laptop. "We'll have to keep an eye on the knee. It's nothing that requires surgery, but it might if you push it too hard. No one wants that. We need you fighting fit and able to kneel." I glanced over at him and winked.

"I like it better when *you* kneel," he said. He rolled his lips and looked towards the open doorway. "Skinner is keeping busy."

"Yes, he's hardly ever in here," I said. "He spends most of his time at the pool. It's me and Doctor Stuart in here, usually." The other doctor was absent at the moment, consulting with the physical therapy team.

"I don't like him being out of sight," Ramsey said. "Don't like him here with you either though."

"He's certainly no fan of mine." I pressed the return button and closed the laptop.

"Maybe you should make him one," Ramsey said. "Make him trust you."

"I don't know if it would be that easy." I leaned my shoulder against the wall. "He's not the trusting kind. And Dominic King knows who my brother is. They're probably watching me as close as I'm watching them."

Ramsey looked thoughtful. "We can use that. Make them think they see things that aren't there. Feed them wrong information."

I bit my lip for a moment. "I guess I could do that. As long as we're careful."

He took a couple of steps towards me. "Always careful." He brushed hair off the side of my face. "If they try anything, they'll regret it."

"I don't mind them having regrets," I said softly. "I don't want to have any myself. I don't want anything to happen to any of you. Working here is amazing, but I feel like I'm in the middle of the hornet's nest."

"You're not, they are," he said. "Soon, they'll get stung. If I could, I'd clear them out now." He looked frustrated, his brow creased, mouth turned down.

"We need to know who they're working for first," I said. Otherwise, I'd be in full agreement about getting rid of both men, and anyone working with them. We could clear out the nest and make it safe for all of us.

Right now, that could bring down more hell on our heads. That would suck.

"Yep," he said simply. "We don't know how deep this goes."

"How deep do you think it goes?" I asked. Several new people started working at the stadium in the last couple of weeks, including a new personal assistant for the GM. I had no idea where the former PA went. One day she was there, the next she was replaced. They could be slowly moving their people in, ready to... I didn't know what. Something that wouldn't be good.

"Deep enough," he said. "We can deal with it. When the time is right. Try to be nice to Otis Skinner. I'll work on some misinformation for you to feed him. Something to give a clue who he's allied with."

"I'm always nice," I said tartly. "But I can be nice to him if it'll end all of this sooner and with less blood being shed." That was what mattered more than anything. Preventing anyone I cared about from being killed. I'd be Otis' best friend to keep everyone safe.

"Not too nice." His brows dipped, gaze firm and intense.

"I'm not planning to add him to the family," I said. "I'm not planning to fuck him either."

If I did, would that help the situation? Would my guys and I be safer if I spent a night with him? Potentially, but the guys would tear him apart if he touched me. Not to mention the idea was repugnant.

If he'd come to Flirts and paid to fuck me, what would I have done then? He gave me the creeps from the moment we met, so I might have found a way to avoid being with him. Divina always gave us a choice. No one was allowed to force us to do anything we weren't comfortable with. I was always grateful for that.

"Of course not," Ramsey agreed. "You're ours. We're not sharing you with anyone else, for any reason. I'll fuck him before I let you do it, and I'm not into other guys."

"I think we've established that none of us is going there," I said. "I'll be friendly, that's all." His possessiveness was hot. Not to mention his admission that he'd sacrifice himself before he'd offer me up. Many others in our lifestyle wouldn't do the same. They wouldn't care if they threw their girlfriends to the lion, as long as it served their purpose.

"Good." He cupped my cheek and leaned in to brush his lips over mine. "I don't want to cut his cock off."

"You sure about that?" I teased. If there was

anything these guys had in common, it was their enjoyment of violence. Whether it was killing or tackling, or being tackled, they loved it.

Storm, in particular, wasn't happy unless he and the people around him were covered in bruises. Me and Frost especially. I wondered what he'd be doing if he wasn't playing rugby. He might have been dragged into this life before now. He probably would have embraced it wholeheartedly.

Ramsey twisted his lips to one side. "Not really," he admitted. "Anyone who touches you that shouldn't, I'll enjoy hurting."

"That was what I thought," I said. "Have you ever —" I glanced toward the doorway. He'd checked the place carefully and there were no listening devices, but I never knew when someone might walk in and overhear.

I whispered in his ear. "Killed anyone." I half-expected someone to hear anyway, but we were alone. No crowd of people came running through the door, shouting at me for asking him a question like that. The world didn't even end.

He whispered back. "Yes. Once. They tried to cross the Brantley family. They regretted it." He leaned back, his expression rueful. Eyes slightly glazed as he thought back to what he did.

"I bet they did," I said.

As far as I knew, that left Storm and Jay who hadn't killed anyone. Jay was more of a mystery to me than some of the other guys, but if Storm had taken a life, he'd say so. That wasn't a thing he'd hold back, especially after Frost killed Ivy. Was he willing to do it? To end someone's life?

I suspected he was. I didn't think he'd hesitate if it was something that had to happen, for my sake or that of any of the guys. I doubted he'd regret it either. Storm was the kind of guy to act first and own it later.

"Did you enjoy it?" I asked carefully. I didn't know why I wanted to know, but I did. Maybe I was just curious about that aspect of his past and personality. How much like the other guys was he?

"Not really," he said. "I don't get off on it like Frost and your brother. It's just a thing that has to be done. I'd be okay if I didn't do it again, but I could if I had to." He cocked his head at me. "Have you ever?"

"Never," I said quickly. "I don't want to either." The idea turned my stomach.

Worse than that, I was scared I'd enjoy it and want to do it again. I was supposed to heal people, not end their lives, but I shared DNA with someone who loved killing. What if I got a taste for it and didn't want to stop? What if I needed to kill like I needed to breathe? I might become addicted to it. The idea was horrifying. I didn't want that to be my life.

"I'll do my best to make sure you don't have to," he assured me. "But if you have to, you can't hesitate."

That scared me too. That I might freak out and not be able to pull the trigger. That my hesitation could get me, and the people I cared about, killed. If anything happened to any of them because I didn't have the guts to do what I had to do, I'd never be able to forgive myself. Especially if I was dead.

"I know," I whispered. "I like to think I can do it if I have to. I know how." Between growing up here and going to Brutham Academy, I learnt several ways to take a life. But like performing surgery, knowing how and actually doing it were different things. Freezing under either circumstance would be bad.

"You can," he said. "You're Chelsea fucking Miller, you can do anything."

I gave him a cheeky smile. "*Doctor* Chelsea fucking Miller," I reminded him. It wasn't that I thought he'd forgotten, but I'd worked hard to get the title, so why not own the fuck out of it?

He snorted softly. "Doctor Chelsea Miller, brat."

"Are you going to punish me?" I looked at him sidelong.

"Yes, but not here," he said. "I have to get back to training, and you to work."

I sighed. "Tease. You're right though, we need to get back to it. But do not overdo the exercise." I shook my finger at him.

"You going to punish me?" His eyes shone. He seemed keen to explore that. Interesting. As I got to know these guys, I saw different sides to them. I had a feeling I could spend the rest of my life with them and still not know everything. That would keep things interesting, for sure.

"Absolutely," I said in my version of a growly voice. "That'll have to wait until later too."

He grimaced, the front of his pants tenting. "Later."

"Later," I agreed. It was going to be a long afternoon.

Chapter Nineteen

Chelsea

After Ramsey left, I headed to the elevators that took me down to the pool a couple of levels below. This was a recently renovated part of the stadium. An old pool replaced with a longer, better one. It shared the space with the physical therapy rooms and a sauna. Nothing but the best for the Dusk Bay Smashers.

I pushed through the glass doors, into the steamy pool room.

Doctor Otis Skinner was overseeing a couple of players walking back and forth up and down the pool to strengthen muscles without putting pressure on their joints.

I stood and watched for a while, admiring the

way they pushed through the water, forcing their way past gallons of pressure without slowing.

"Something I can do for you?" Skinner said after a handful of minutes.

"I'm fascinated by your work," I said. "I was hoping to learn more about it." Of course, we covered aqua therapy at university and I worked with it before, but if he had new, more effective methods, I wanted to understand them.

He responded with a disbelieving side eye. "I don't want you overextending yourself. You're still settling into the job."

"It's never too early to avoid getting stale," I said easily. "Especially with something as fascinating as what you're working on." Which he hadn't elaborated on. Apart from reading his paper on the benefit of aqua therapy on muscle strain, I didn't know exactly what his angle was.

A suspicious person might think he didn't have one. Me, I'd give him the benefit of the doubt. For now.

He grunted. "Very well. Let's not speak over the pool."

"Of course." I stepped over to stand beside him. "What have you been working on, Doctor Skinner?" I asked politely.

"You may call me Otis," he said. "I've been working on the impact of water therapy on players' mental health. Using a combination of Watsu and Bad Ragaz methods. They combine exercise with immersion in the water. Usually, one of us would be in the water with them, supporting them as they do their movements."

I had to admit, I was impressed. The players' mental health was important, but sometimes I felt like it was put aside to focus on physical health and fitness.

"I love that," I said sincerely. "I don't think there's too many people who aren't more relaxed and comfortable after floating in water."

"Precisely," he said. "I believe pool therapy could replace gym exercise, if undertaken correctly. Water is a much more flexible medium, and less inclined to damage the body."

Unless someone was held under for too long, I thought.

"I'd imagine the coaching staff has different thoughts about that," I said. "They seem to like having the guys do laps on the field."

"I prefer they do laps in the pool," he said. "They'd find their performance to be positively impacted by my methods."

"Will they let you test that theory?" I asked. In order to do that, some of the guys would only exercise with his methods, while the others used the gym and field.

"With the junior division," he said, looking irritated. "When my methods have proven sound, they'll consent to expanding the program." He seemed very sure of that. Of course, there was nothing wrong with backing his own work. Why do all the study if he didn't believe in his own findings?

"In that case, I'm on the right side of history if I learn more from you," I said. "It sounds to me like you're doing important work." Under other circumstances, I'd be behind him completely. As it was, I felt uncomfortable standing next to him and a body of water. Not that I thought he'd try anything with this many witnesses in the area right now.

"I am," he said with an edge of reluctance. Reluctance to share too much more information with me? Or maybe he didn't want to share with anyone? He might be scared I'd try to steal his work somehow. Or insinuate myself into his studies so my name would be included in anything he published. It happened often enough.

"Ramsey is working with you, isn't he?" I said with some reluctance of my own. "I get the impression he's been doing too much. Pool therapy might be better than spending so much time in the gym."

"He has been working with me," Otis agreed. He looked at me carefully, as if trying to figure out whether or not I caught on to his double meaning.

I pretended to be completely oblivious. "I'm worried he's working himself too hard," I said. "I just saw him and looked at his knee. According to his notes, you've been doing the same. How does he seem to you?"

I hated talking about Ramsey behind his back, but if he wasn't going to open up to me about why he was working out too hard, maybe Otis could give me some insight. If we bonded over this, he might come to trust me.

"As you say, he's been over-exercising," Otis said. "I've insisted he do more pool work, especially Watsu, but he's resistant. I believe he thinks relaxing is counter-productive."

"That sounds like every guy on the team," I said dryly. "They like to be busy. Active." Of course they did; they were all physical guys. None of them would be happy sitting in an office day after day. They liked to be on the go as much as they could.

"Indeed," Otis agreed. "The support of their coach would be helpful."

"You think if Coach Stanley ordered them to do more in the pool, they would? I mean, of course they would, but with his backing they might be less resistant?" I assumed that was what he was getting at.

"Precisely." He nodded. "They understand its benefits as a treatment, but as an exercise regime in and of itself? That's where they are most reluctant. They're accustomed to stationary bikes and treadmills."

"So, you think pool therapy is a holistic approach?" I said. "Body and mind."

"That's exactly what it is," he said. "Fortunately, the GM believes as I do. He may consider replacing Coach Stanley with someone who supports my work and my methods."

There was a double meaning in that too. He wanted the head coach replaced with someone who was working with them outside of working with the team. If Coach Stanley wasn't careful, he'd end up like Bruce Fergus, but courtesy of Otis instead of Atlas.

"I'm sure Coach Stanley could be coerced," I said carefully. "If he understood what was at stake, he might change his mind." I sent a mental apology to the head coach. Their kind of coercion would suck. No doubt they'd already considered it, but I was trying to get Skinner on my side. The guys would have to do whatever was necessary to keep the coach from ending up dead.

"Most people can be coerced," Otis said meaningfully. "I would have thought you were the 'have a pleasant conversation with someone' kind of woman. Hope to convince them to rethink."

"I am that kind of woman," I agreed. "But sometimes, things have to be taken a step further. For the good of the team," I added quickly.

"Of course, for the good of the team," he agreed. "If you had to coerce him, what would you suggest?"

This was a test, and I wasn't sure if I could pass. If I was honest, I wasn't sure I wanted to. I waded in this far, I might as well press on. We both knew what was going on here. More or less.

"That depends how resistant he is," I said. "Brutham Academy taught several different varieties of coercion. Beyond that, I know people. I'm sure you do too."

"I might, but I'm more interested to hear about you," he said. He was still sceptical, wondering what my angle was. Men like him didn't get far by trusting one casual conversation. "I'm aware who your brother is and who he works for."

"That's him," I said. "I make up my own mind

about who I work with. For the record, my brother gets restless. He doesn't always agree with his boss. Like most people, he's always wanting to expand his power."

"Interesting," Otis said.

"I thought so," I said. If he really thought my brother would turn his back on his boss, he was mistaken, but he didn't need to know that. Not right now anyway. If he believed we'd flip and work with him, that would work in our favour.

"We might need to test this theory," he said slowly. "Find out how much coercion is necessary."

I looked over to him. "Did you have something in mind?"

He looked back at me. "How do I know I can trust you?"

"Ramsey trusts me," I said. "Who do you think sent me here?" I made a note to tell Ramsey I brought him into the conversation. No doubt Otis would ask him directly. I was sure he could handle himself, but it would help if he wasn't taken by surprise.

"Ferris Ramsey sent his girlfriend to me?" Otis mused. "That is interesting. He was instrumental in uncovering a mole." Apparently he bought Ramsey's story about the way she died.

I had a feeling he didn't know Dallas' part in it. I

hoped like hell he didn't. Dallas had been through enough already. I didn't want him to become more of a target than any of us already were.

"India," I said. "She was always tight with the Brantley family. They must have thought she could fool you." She couldn't deny that accusation, but it gave him something to think about.

"I wonder the same about you," he said smoothly. "Your family is tight with the Brantleys too." He seemed to have done his homework when it came to all of us. I wouldn't have expected anything else from him. Taking chances could get you dead too easily.

"In the past," I agreed. "Like I said, things change. We've been under their thumb for a long time. That's started to chafe. Ramsey and I agree on that. I'm sure we could convince my brother and his partners. If the price was right."

This whole conversation began to make me sick. I felt like I was digging myself deeper and deeper into a hole, getting more involved with the life I tried so hard to avoid. I wanted to hop on a plane and hide in one of those cottages in New Zealand. Somewhere no one could find me but my guys.

I didn't run. I stood my ground. There was more at stake than me and my sanity. If I could go along with him for a little while, I could find out everything we needed to know. Or put Ramsey in a position where he could learn more. Either way, it was a sacrifice I had to make.

"I'll talk to my boss and consider your proposal," he said. "Your brother would be a valuable asset to us. As would you. If you can be trusted."

"I could say the same to you," I said. "How do I know you won't stab me in the back the moment I look away?" If he knew what was going on in my mind, he would. If I didn't get to him first.

This was a very dangerous knife edge I was walking on. One slip and I'd be sliced open, from head to toe. Possibly literally.

"You don't," he said. "I may give you a chance to prove yourself. If you can show your loyalty, you'll have nothing to worry about."

He didn't need to add the words, 'and if you can't, you'll be dead.' They hung right there in the steamy air between us.

Chapter Twenty

Atlas

I scowled through the glass doors as Chelsea and Otis Skinner talked.

"They look cosy," Jay said from beside me. He looked as irritated as I felt, his jaw clenched tight.

"They're—" I started, my face heating with anger.

He held up his hands. "I know they're not, I meant she's doing a good job looking like they are. I'd be a nervous wreck."

He looked ready to punch me if I came at him. I wouldn't. I never had. I must have looked angrier than I thought.

"No, you wouldn't." I blew a couple of breaths in and out, calming myself. Okay, trying to. I didn't want to be angry at him, especially for something so stupid. I misinterpreted what he meant. That was my bad.

Seeing Chelsea so close to the enemy made me want to lose my shit. I wanted to run in there, push him in the pool and hold him under until his body went still. Dominic King with him. As well as anyone else who thought they could fuck with my woman.

"I'm sorry." Jay took a step back. "I didn't mean to stir the pot."

"You didn't, it's me," I said. "I'm edgy as fuck right now. When this started, it was just you and me and that was bad enough. Now everyone is getting dragged into it. I can't..." I shook my head. "I can't keep everyone safe. I don't know if I can keep you safe, or her."

I looked back to her as she smiled at something Skinner said. It wasn't her sincere, genuinely happy smile, but him making her smile at all pissed me off. I didn't care if it was fake; it still drove me crazy.

It occurred to me they might ask her to sleep with him. That thought enraged me more than anything else.

The thought of her fucking so many men before I came along was bad enough, but anyone else except us touching her now... I wanted to rip him apart so he couldn't go near her. There was no way in hell I was letting his cock anywhere near her pussy. Her body belonged to us. She belonged to us. End of story, no matter what the consequences were. Even if we all ended up dead, it would be better than letting her be fucked by him.

"I've noticed," Jay said. "So am I. On edge, I mean."

That made me stop and look over at him. "I know you are. I should have tried to keep you out of this." I should have tried to keep all of them out of this. If I hadn't been so quick to kill Bruce Fergus, maybe I could have.

I was thinking clearly at the time, but hadn't thought it all the way through, or I might have let him live. Chelsea would have ended up working somewhere else, away from the craziness. We'd still be together, I'd make sure of that, but she wouldn't be standing there right now, having a conversation with someone who would kill us without hesitation.

Jay snorted. "Yeah, right. How would you have done that? I'm involved because I wanted to be involved. Remember? I can think for myself, you know."

He seemed annoyed, defensive, the vein in his forehead throbbing. Like somehow I was treating him like a kid. I knew plenty of people in his past did exactly that. I always tried not to. He hadn't been a kid for a long time. Just because he was on the spectrum didn't mean he deserved to be treated like one. He was intelligent, loyal and devoted to the game.

I meant it when I said he was special. He was one of the best people I ever met. I wanted to kick myself for making him feel otherwise.

"I know you can." I put a hand on his shoulder. "You're right, you would have been up to your eyeballs, no matter what I said. If I hadn't come, you would have left me behind."

"Naw, I wouldn't." He put a hand over mine. "We're in this together. You, me, Chelsea, Frost and the others. No one is responsible for anyone else, or everyone else. Not even you."

"Not even Storm?" I asked jokingly.

"Not even him," Jay agreed. "He's a bossy prick, but we still have minds of our own. Most of us anyway." He managed a grin.

"You definitely do," I said. I gave his shoulder a squeeze and dropped my hand to my side. "What do you think of all of this?" I should have asked him that sooner.

"I think I'd like to go for a swim," he said. "That water looks inviting." He slid a look towards Skinner, his expression suggesting he was thinking the same thing I was.

"It does," I agreed. "But you don't need to be the one to do it."

"Maybe I want to?" he suggested. "It seems like a rite of passage." He could have been talking about giving someone a wedgie, or filling their locker with confetti. The usual dumb things people used to do when hazing was allowed.

Now, they were relegated to practical jokes amongst friends, and then used with discretion.

They weren't on the same playing field as killing people.

"It's not," I said. "Trust me, it's not something you want to start doing." Every time I killed someone, I felt like I gave up another piece of my soul. I didn't regret it, but it ate away at me anyway. Reminding me I was human, more or less.

"I might have to," he said. "If I do, then I do. I'm not afraid of it." He lifted his stubbled chin defiantly. Braver than I might have been if the tables were turned. If I knew then what I know now, I would have given serious thought to walking away before I made my first kill.

I fixed him with a steady look. "You should be. It shouldn't be a thing you look forward to doing."

"What if I am?" he asked. He looked anxious now, his eyes averted to the side of my face.

"It won't change how I feel about you," I said quietly. "But I promise, it will change how you feel about yourself. I don't want that for you."

"Do you want it for Storm?" he asked.

"I don't want it for anyone," I said. "Not even him. Not even for Otis Skinner or anyone like him. It fucks you up. It starts to make you think like it's a solution to every problem when it's not."

Okay, that depended on the problem, but I couldn't kill everyone who pissed me off, or there'd be no one left. I'd start with people who pulled out of the side streets in front of my car, then go really slowly. Next up would be anyone who pushes in line. I really hated when people did that.

"You can't change it if it has to happen," he said.

"I know, but I'll be there for you if it does," I said. "I'll be there for Chelsea if she has to do it, too." I knew she liked all of this even less than I did. I hated that she'd been dragged back into this when she'd worked so hard to get out and make her own life.

As far as I could tell, it was inevitable, in spite of what she thought or wanted. She was a mafia princess, even if she didn't want to admit it.

"Will you be there for Storm?" Jay asked. "If it fucks him up, will you be there to hold his hand?"

"If I have to," I said. I didn't think he'd want me to. He was the kind of guy who'd hide behind a mask, pretending he was fine when he wasn't. When he was alone, he'd quietly fall apart. He'd try to, anyway. Now, he had us to look out for him. Whether he liked it or not.

"I'm not going to kiss his boo-boo better," I added. "He has Chelsea and Frost for that."

Jay grinned. "I think he'd kick your ass if you tried to kiss his boo-boo."

"I'd kick my own ass," I said. "I'm particular about whose boo-boo I kiss."

"Me too," Jay agreed. "Although, Storm has a nice-looking boo-boo." He raised his eyebrows and gave me a sly look, deliberately stirring the pot.

"Should I be jealous?" I asked jokingly. As if I ever had reason to be jealous of Storm Keller.

"Naw, I like yours better," he said. He turned from me to look back at Chelsea. "Speaking of cute boo-boos, it looks like they're done in there."

I followed his gaze. Chelsea walked away from Skinner, her back rigid. She looked as though she was having the same thoughts as us. She could turn around now and give him a quick shove—

She didn't. She walked to the door and pushed out, smiling when she saw us. She kept walking until we were around the corner and out of sight of Skinner.

"Hey." She gave us a quick kiss each, trying not to display too much affection in our workplace. For far too many reasons, it was better not to draw too much attention to us.

"You good?" I put a hand on her lower back and guided her towards the elevator.

"Yeah," she said. "Doctor Skinner has some interesting theories. Some that could be quite beneficial to the team." She spoke lightly, like she was genuinely impressed, and the conversation went well. As if it was nothing more than one professional consulting with another. As if one conversation couldn't get people killed.

"Others not?" Jay guessed, keeping it vague.

"Let's say he has some interesting ideas," she said. "I look forward to learning more."

The elevator pinged and the doors opened. We stepped inside and waited for them to close behind us. Only once they had, I put my arm around her. She leaned against me, giving and taking comfort.

On the outside, she was tough as hell, but on the inside she needed all the support she could get. Like the rest of us, she used a mask to pretend she was okay when she wasn't. Here, when it was only the three of us, she didn't need to pretend.

"What the hell?" I asked.

In a handful of sentences, she told me about her conversation with Ramsey, then with Otis.

"Fuck," Jay whispered. "They don't mean coerced, do they? They mean kill. Coach Stanley is the best coach the Smashers ever had."

"They don't care about winning," she said. "Not rugby, anyway. The team is just a means to an end. A cover for what they're really doing."

"We can't get him involved," I said. "As far as I know, he has no idea about any of this."

"If it's the only way to bring down the enemy..." Jay said slowly.

I stared at him, and shook my head. "That's where it starts. Innocent people like him get involved and then everything is fucked."

"What choice do we have?" Jay asked. "If he asks Chelsea and Ice to do something to him to prove their loyalty, what are they supposed to do?"

I held Chelsea tighter. "I don't know. What would Ice do?"

"He wouldn't like to torture an innocent man, but if it was necessary in order to bring down Otis,

Dominic King and Carlos Jones, then..." She looked like she was struggling to hold herself together.

"Does he need to be tortured?" I said slowly. "They might just want him killed and gotten out of the way."

She looked at me, blue eyes glistening. "What are you saying?" she whispered.

"I'm saying, I have an idea. In the meantime, we have to act normally. Relax and wait until things play out. You're finished for the day, right?"

She nodded. "Right."

"Good, then let's go home."

Chapter Twenty-One

Chelsea

"Can't sleep either?" Frost poured himself a drink of water and swallowed it down in one gulp. Wearing only a pair of exercise shorts and messy hair, he looked adorable. Good enough to eat.

"It seems to be contagious," I said. "Did I wake you?"

"I wasn't asleep," he said. "I saw you slip out of the bedroom and wanted to make sure you were okay."

"As okay as I can be under the circumstances," I said with a sigh. "With everything that's going on, my brain won't slow down."

He put his empty glass in the dishwasher and stepped over to wrap his arms around me. "Believe it or not, mine won't either."

I rested my head against his bare chest. "Why wouldn't I believe it?"

"I dunno," he said. "Some people think I'm, I don't know, shallow or something. Like all there is to me is muscles and playing footy."

"They don't know you very well, then," I said. "You're as smart as you are sweet."

He pulled his face back and looked at me, pretending to be offended. "Hey!"

I slapped him lightly on the chest. "You are sweet, Daniel Frost. And smart. If I ever hear you say otherwise again, I'm going to kick your ass."

"Now who's threatening who with a good time?" he teased. He slipped his hands down the back of my sleep shorts and squeezed my ass. "We could start here."

"Do you trust me?" I asked.

He looked surprised, but nodded without hesitation. "Of course I do. Why? Are you up to something?" He didn't seem too concerned.

"I might be." I grabbed his wrist to pull his hands out of my shorts and kissed both of his palms, one after the other. Giving him a sly smile, I led him over to the door, grabbing my phone on the way out. I sent a quick text to the group chat, so none of the guys would worry about where we were.

"I guess that would be a yes," Frost said, smiling easily. "Lucky for me, I'd follow you anywhere. Where are we going?"

"You'll see." We headed over to the elevators and took the car down one floor. The doors slid open to show Atlas standing outside, waiting for us. Like Frost, he was only dressed in a pair of shorts, his hair sticking out in all directions.

"I think I like where this is going," Frost said. "Let me guess, you've brought me down here for a classic animated series marathon."

"Fuck no," Atlas said. He grimaced at Frost before leading us down the corridor and unlocking the door to his apartment.

"Then we must be here for a sleepover," Frost said.

"Sleep might be involved eventually," I agreed. I took Frost's hand and we walked behind Atlas to the bedroom he shared with Jay.

Jay sat in the middle of the bed, completely naked.

"You have the best ideas," Frost said to me. He didn't bother to hide his admiring gaze.

"Yeah, I do," I agreed. I slipped out of my pyjamas and left them on the floor.

"Wait." Atlas caught my wrist. "Frost, you can get

naked too." He slid out of his own pants and kicked them off.

Frost eyed him, but hurried to comply.

"Both of you, get on the edge of the bed and crawl to Jay," Atlas said.

I exchanged glances and smiles with Frost before we knelt together and started to crawl, both with our eyes on Jay. My breasts swung with each slow, deliberate movement.

Jay's eyes were wide and dark, like he didn't know where to look. His gaze swivelled from me, to Frost, to Atlas and back again. His cock was hard, pointing toward the ceiling.

I stopped in front of him and sat down before looking back at Atlas. If he decided to take the lead tonight, I'd let him have it. The others seemed content with that too. As content as two aroused men with thick erections could be.

"Jay and Frost, I want to see you together," Atlas said after a few moments thought. "I want you to fuck each other." He sat on the end of the bed and watched as they reached for each other, lips meeting, hard body against hard body.

The moans they made as they kissed and stroked each other's cocks were arousing as hell. Even more so when Jay took a tube of lube from the bedside table. He waited until Frost turned his back to him and smeared it around Frost's rear hole.

He knelt behind Frost and carefully stretched him with his fingers, eyes glazed with concentration, before replacing them with his cock.

Frost's eyes crossed in bliss as Jay started to slowly thrust in and out of him.

"Lie back," Atlas said to me. When I did, he lay over me, his knees to either side. He nudged the tip of his cock against my entrance before sliding into my wet heat.

It was my turn for my eyes to cross in bliss. As long as I lived, I'd never get enough of the way their cocks felt inside me. So perfect, like all six of them were made for me. And for each other.

I watched Jay thoroughly fuck Frost as Atlas fucked me. Side-by-side, matching thrust for thrust. Moans and groans of pleasure mingling together in the night.

Jay was the first to come, crying out as he ground into Frost. His grunts and groans pushed me over the edge into an orgasm. More soft and gentle than hard and intense, but no less pleasurable.

Atlas came a few moments later, buried deep inside my body. He sagged, panting for a few moments before rolling off me. "Frost, I want to see you fuck Chelsea."

Frost didn't need to be told twice. He scrambled over to claim Atlas's spot over me, quickly sliding himself into me, my channel slick with my release and Atlas'.

He pumped into me, hard and fast, relentless to the point of desperation. Driving me, pushing me until I came again, shouting his name to the ceiling so loud my throat felt raw. Loud enough to wake Ramsey, and the rest of the building.

Frost was quick to follow, coming inside me, as he grunted. "Fuck...yeah...so fucking good. So... ahhhh." He fell still, eyes half closed in concentration as he came, adding his release to Atlas'. Slowly rolling his hip, grinding into me to draw out every drop of his orgasm. "Fucking incredible."

Hands on either side of me, he sagged forward, panting until he was able to catch his breath. He slid himself out of me and flopped down beside me. "Woman, you are everything."

"Jay, clean her up with your mouth," Atlas said.

Eyes wide, Jay hurried to dive down between my thighs. His eyes on me, he started to lick away Atlas and Frost's cum.

My pussy was sensitive so soon after coming, but he was as relentless as the others, lapping at me and sucking my clit, teasing my piercing with his lips and tongue. He glanced up at me, eyes smiling. He wasn't stopping until I came again, no matter how long it took.

I smiled back and tilted my head, looking up at the ceiling while I let myself enjoy the way he was pushing me on and on, higher and higher. Closer, so close...

"I'm going to come," I whispered.

"Do it," Atlas ordered. "Come for us."

"Yes, come for us," Frost agreed. Apparently Storm, Atlas and Ramsey were rubbing off on him. Literally and figuratively.

I looked over at him, but he just grinned and nodded for me to obey. Who was I to argue?

Jay didn't let up. He didn't even slow. He went on licking and sucking my clit until I came against his mouth, this time hard and so intense it was all I knew for at least a minute or two.

Universes were born and died in a shower of stars and fireworks before I slowly came back down and flopped boneless on the mattress.

"Is this where the sleep part comes in?" Frost asked, covering a yawn with his hand.

"For now," Atlas agreed. "Get some rest, you're all going to need it."

Chapter Twenty-Two

Chelsea

I WAS STILL ON A HIGH FROM THE NIGHT BEFORE, when I got a text on my phone that Dominic King wanted to see me. That was all, just a text. At my earliest convenience, please. At least he was polite. Or his PA was, anyway.

The high ended abruptly. Of course reality had to crash back down, it always did.

Doctor Stuart must have seen my face, because he was looking over the top of his laptop, his eyebrows raised. "Anything wrong?"

"The GM wants to see me." I tucked my phone into my pocket and started to turn back to reorganising files on my laptop. Doctor Stuart was good at a lot of things, but he handed this over to me because it wasn't one of them.

"Then you go," he waved me away. "That can wait until later."

I started to shut down my laptop. Grateful, because I didn't want to spend the next hour or two wondering what King had to say. "Do you have any idea what this is about?"

"Not a clue," Doctor Stuart said. "I'm guessing he's not planning to fire you, because he would have mentioned that to me first."

I wasn't sure if that was the case, but I was grateful for the reassurance. If nothing else, it settled my racing heart a little. Of course, King could be asking me up to his office to kill me, but that wouldn't be subtle. Me going missing in the middle of the day would not go unnoticed.

"I'll try not to be long." I pulled my phone out again and shot a quick text off to the group chat I had with the guys, to let them know where I was going. If I did go missing, they'd know where to start looking and pointing fingers.

Before any of them could answer, I put my phone away and headed down to the elevators. After what felt like days of waiting, the doors finally opened and I stepped inside. I pressed the button to take me two floors higher and practiced my breathing exercises while the carriage rose.

The doors finally slid open and I stepped out, my heels clicking on the floor as I made my way to the desk in front of the GM's office. The woman who sat behind the desk reminded me of the teapot in *Beauty and the Beast*. Older, motherly. Not the kind of person I would have expected to find here. Which was probably the point.

"Doctor Chelsea Miller, to see the GM," I said. "He wanted to see me?"

"Oh yes, sweetie," she said, adding to the whole motherly vibe. If she was the kind of woman Dominic King would hire, maybe I was wrong about him. Or maybe she was here to confuse people like me. Throw us off so we weren't on guard around him. Unfortunately for him, I wasn't that naïve.

"Please, go on in." She half-rose and waved towards the door. "It shouldn't take too long. It better not, or I'll shake my finger at him again for working too hard." She finished with a laugh.

"We wouldn't want that," I said. I reminded myself she was probably the enemy and would be as likely to wave a gun at me as a finger. I stepped over to the door and pushed the rest of the way open.

"You wanted to see me?" I asked.

He held up a finger and listened to the phone

that was pressed against his ear. "Make sure it gets done," he said. "Yes, that's right. Good." Without saying goodbye, he ended the call. He set the phone down on the desk beside his laptop and steepled his fingers.

"Close the door."

I took a step back and did as he asked, keeping my eyes on him the whole time. He wasn't someone I'd comfortably turn my back on. Although, if I did, I wouldn't have to see the calculating look in his eyes.

"Have a seat." He nodded to the chair opposite him.

Slowly, I sank down into it, my hands in my lap. If I looked non-threatening, maybe he'd be the same. I got the impression he wasn't about to pull out a gun and use it on me. No, whatever he wanted was worse than that.

"How are you settling in?" he asked.

Oh good, small talk.

I managed a smile. "Really well, thank you. What about you? How are you finding managing the Smashers?" It didn't hurt to be nice, right?

"Interesting and stimulating," he said. "I'd imagine you've found it the same?"

"Definitely," I said. I was pretty sure I found it

interesting and stimulating in very different ways to him, but it was both of those things. "It's been everything I hoped it would be and more. Every day is a new challenge."

"Indeed." He inclined his head. "Each day, I don't know what I'll be faced with. It keeps things fresh and all of us on our toes."

"I feel exactly the same," I said carefully. "I love working for the team."

"I haven't brought you here to fire you," he said. "Quite the opposite."

That was a relief. Wasn't it? On second thought, what was the opposite of being fired? I wasn't quite sure. I had a feeling I wasn't going to like it, but I threw my hat in the ring by talking to Otis Skinner. Sooner or later this conversation was going to happen.

"That's great," I said. "What did you have in mind? I don't think Doctor Stuart is ready to retire yet." *That* might be the opposite of being fired. It seemed unlikely he'd promote me instead of Otis Skinner. A girl could dream, right?

"I trust he isn't," King agreed. "His expertise is invaluable to the team."

I was relieved to hear that. Apparently Doctor Stuart wasn't getting in their way. Not yet, at least.

"It really is," I agreed. "I've learned so much from him and Doctor Skinner. I'm lucky to be able to work with both of them." Was I gushing? A little bit. Maybe I shouldn't lay it on so thick.

"Doctor Skinner mentioned your interest in his work," King said smoothly. "He suggested you might wish to become more involved. More...hands-on."

I swallowed. "I would," I agreed. Okay, I lied through my teeth. "If his work is the way of the future, I'd rather be on board now than...become obsolete." No doubt he'd follow my double meaning.

"You really think that'll happen?" he asked.

"Plenty of people have placed bets on the wrong team," I said. "They tend to regret it. I want to put my money on the *right* team. When the game is over, I want to be standing on the field, celebrating the win, not crying over the loss."

He nodded slowly. "I always find it wiser to back the right team. Some people believe, because a team has always taken the cup, they always will."

"That's naïve," I said. In football and in life. No one won all the time. "Especially when the new team has fresh blood and the determination to win. Let the old team get complacent. They'll realise their mistake eventually."

"You think the Brantley family has become complacent?" he asked bluntly.

"Why wouldn't they?" I asked without blinking. "It's been years since anyone truly opposed them. Who wouldn't get complacent? If anyone was going to take advantage of that, now would be the time. But that's just my opinion." I sat back.

"I'm of the same opinion," he said. "I think your brother, you and your boyfriends will be useful to me. The question is, can I trust any of you?"

"I could ask you the same thing," I said. He'd be expecting me to say something like that. If I was too willing to jump straight in, he'd be suspicious.

"That remains to be seen," he said. "I have a job for you. If you can carry it out, I may have more." He leaned forward, propping his elbows on the desk. "I happen to agree that the Brantley family has become complacent. We'll show them the consequences of that. There's power to be taken and we're going to take it."

I smiled. "As long as you leave some of it for me. And my brother. Believe me when I say things won't end well if you try to leave him out of it. There's not much he wouldn't do."

"I'd expect nothing less of Doctor Isaac Miller,"

King said. "I'd much prefer to work with him than have to have him killed."

As if killing my brother would be easy. I tried to keep most of the scorn off my face. A fraction of it would be okay. I was supposed to have faith in me and my brother, so he'd be expecting that exact response.

"He'd also prefer that," I said. "Working with you instead of having to kill you." I smiled sweetly. I didn't want him to think I was threatening him. I was just stating a fact.

He actually smiled. "You have some backbone. I like that. Do you have enough of it to do what I'm going to ask you to do?"

I met his gaze unwavering. "I have the spine, if it's in my best interest to do what you request." I wasn't going to say, 'yes sir, no sir' and behave myself like a good little minion. Even after trying to stay out of the lifestyle, I had some clout. My brother had even more. Enough that we didn't have to roll over and play dead. If we did that, King would try to walk all over us. That wasn't going to happen.

Not to mention that none of my guys, or my brother, would go for it anyway.

King didn't flinch. "Otis Skinner mentioned you discussed Coach Stanley with him."

"That's right," I inclined my head slightly. "He suggested Stanley doesn't agree with the direction you want the team to go."

"He doesn't, and I don't believe he'll come around to our way of thinking," King said. "I want him taken care of."

I blinked. "I see. You want me to take care of him."

That was fucking perfect, wasn't it? Not.

"If you're up to it," he said. King seemed certain I wasn't and that he was about to call my bluff. That I'd make some excuse and get the hell out of the building. Maybe out of Dusk Bay.

"I'm up to it," I said, also unflinching. "I'll quietly take care of him and leave you to replace him with someone more suitable."

He actually seemed surprised, but rallied quickly. "Good. You have two days. I don't care what you do, but if it can be traced back to me, you'll be the one with regrets."

With more confidence than I felt, I snorted. "This isn't amateur hour. No one will know what really happened to Coach Stanley but us. Nothing will be traceable back to us. No one will have a reason to sniff around, or have suspicions. Except for the short amount of time between the death of the former GM and then the head coach."

"I'm sure you can make it convincing," he said. "That will be all."

Resisting the urge to respond to his curt dismissal, I stood and slipped out of the room.

Chapter Twenty-Three

Atlas

"This is some bullshit," Storm said. He gripped on to the steering wheel of his SUV so tight his knuckles were white.

"Yeah." I couldn't disagree with that statement. "We did what we had to do, though."

"It sucked," he growled. "He was a good man. A good fucking coach. Who are we going to get now, some prick from the Devils? Someone who thinks the sun shines out of his own ass? Someone who got his head up there so hard, he hasn't seen daylight for fuck knows how long?"

"None of the coaches we had were that bad," I argued.

"If they're on Dominic King's side, they're bad,"

he insisted. "If he thinks what we just did is okay, then he's bad."

"I know it sucked, but you have to put a lid on it," I said. "We need them to think we're on their side."

He glanced over to me, then back to the road. "Aren't we? Have you been paying attention for the last few hours? Were you there for what we just did?"

"Yeah, but I'm not gonna get hysterical over it," I said evenly. "It was what it was."

"I'm not hysterical," he snapped. "Don't give me that greater good bullshit, either. It wasn't good for any of us, or the team."

"In the long run it will be," I said. "Look, I get it, you're pissed off. I didn't enjoy it either. For the rest of my life, I'm going to see the expression on his face. Nothing we ever do is going to make it up to him or his family. All we can do is keep on keeping on."

"It's easy for you to say, you've done shit like that before," he said.

"I promise you, it doesn't get easier each time," I said. "It gets harder. Do you think I enjoyed looking Coach Stanley in the eyes and doing that? I didn't. Frost and Dallas, they might have, but not me."

"We could have brought them along to make it easier," Storm said.

"We agreed the more of us that were involved in this, the harder it would be to hide it," I said. "It doesn't matter now; it's done. Yes, we probably will get someone from the Devils. Get used to the idea now, so you don't open your mouth at the wrong time. I don't want to end up dead because you can't contain your shit."

"I can contain my shit," he argued. "If you can contain yours."

"I have a locked box in the back of my brain for my shit," I said. I let out a long, slow breath and looked out the window, watching the dark landscape slide by. "We have to act like nothing's changed between us."

"Nothing has," he said. He shifted his position in the seat and cleared his throat.

"We both know that's not true," I said. "We haven't called each other an asshole for at least an hour."

"Asshole," he said immediately. "Just reminding myself how it felt."

I snorted. "I don't hate you." After a moment I added, "Asshole."

"Of course you do," he said. "Anyone with half a brain hates me. Including myself."

"You should give yourself some credit," I said.

"You're not that bad. Bad, but not *that* bad." I couldn't resist the dig.

"You too, prick," he replied. "Remind me why we got stuck doing this again?"

"Because the others are watching out for Chelsea," I said. "And because we both wanted to spare them from what we did tonight. Frost and Dallas, they enjoy killing, but this was different. Personal."

"Yeah, nothing says personal like taking your head coach out to a remote location and dealing with him," Storm said. His voice broke on the last couple of words. "Like I said, this is some bullshit."

"And we can't talk about it," I reminded him. "Not to the other guys or even Chelsea. The less they know about what we did, the better. Then they don't have to lie."

They could handle themselves, but they didn't have to in this situation. We'd save them from that much.

"Yeah, yeah, I know. Was this some kind of team bonding thing?" he asked. "You could have brought Jay with you. He would have dealt with it."

"I didn't want him to have to," I said. "And I'm not sure he would have. I knew you would."

"Because I'm an asshole," he concluded.

"Because you're a badass," I said. "But if you tell anyone I said that, I'll deny it. The official story is, you're a heartless prick who wouldn't care what happened to his head coach."

"That's not true," he said, his voice smaller than I ever heard before.

"I know that," I said. "I think you put on an act. You want everyone to think Storm Keller, fullback, is bullet-proof and gives no shits about anyone but himself. But underneath, you're the same as the rest of us. You have feelings and shit like that."

"Maybe I do." He shrugged one shoulder, making the car veer slightly. He straightened up and pressed his lips together, his focus back on the road. "I fucking hate what we did. I want to walk into Dominic King's office and wrap my hands around his throat. Then I want to drag Otis Skinner under the water and hold them there for approximately an hour. And everyone else who has anything to do with this crap. You know what?"

"What?" I raised my eyebrows at him questioningly.

"Things were easier when I didn't know anything about this mafia stuff," he said. "My life was all about footy, fucking Chelsea and hanging out with Frosty. Now, I feel like we're some weird version of the

Blues Brothers. We'll get home and find horse heads in our beds."

"I think you might be mixing your movies, but I get your point," I said. "A few weeks ago, you wouldn't have been driving down the highway in the middle of the night, back to Dusk Bay. You would have been at home, watching a movie or seeing how many times you could make our woman come before she couldn't take anymore."

"Exactly," he said with a grunt. "How did we end up here?"

"I think it was something to do with Frost strangling Ivy," I said. "But the minute you got together with Chelsea, at least some of this was inevitable. She denies it, but this is her world. This is mine, now it's yours. I don't think you're planning to walk away from it, are you?"

"I'm not walking away from her," he agreed. "If this is the shit that has to happen, then I guess..." He shook his head. "This is fucked up."

"It is, but we can deal with it," I said.

He barked a laugh. "It's not like we have a choice. Not now. We're in it up to our balls. Our eyeballs, just to be clear."

"Whatever balls you want to bring into the conversation, we're in it up to them," I said. "If we weren't, Chelsea might have had to do this herself. I wouldn't wish that on her. Would you?"

"Hell no," he said immediately. "She'd never forgive herself."

I wasn't sure if that was completely true, but close enough. She was more of a badass than she gave herself credit for. She'd do whatever was necessary, then she'd move on. Like she had from handing Belinda Simmons to her brother to keep everyone from finding out she used to be a stripper. She did it because she had to. When it came down to it, remorse was no use at the best of times. Especially not once the woman was dead.

"Lucky she has us to do that dirty work for her," I said."

"Is that what we are now?" he asked. "Dirty deeds done dirt cheap by Dusk Bay dudes?"

"That can be our tagline," I said. "We could have a van with that down the side." I held up my hands to mime a wide sticker. "Dusk Bay dudes, doing dirty deeds since... Something beginning with D."

He snorted a laugh. "Dusk Bay dickheads, more like it. Dragged into dirty deeds despite demselves."

"To save damsels," I added. "From distress."

"Dat's about right." He nodded, but was trying to hold back a laugh.

"If you're not careful, I'm going to understand what the others see in you," I said. "Not physically; you might be much less of an asshole than I first thought."

"No, I'm as big an asshole as you thought," he said. "I'm just fucking funny sometimes. Don't tell anyone, I don't want them to get some weird expectations about me."

"I won't say a word," I said. He was definitely not that bad, but if he wanted to go on believing he was, there wasn't much I could say to convince him otherwise.

"Good. If you don't, neither will I." He took a breath in through his nose, and out again before he spoke again. "You might not be as bad as I thought you were either. I'm not saying we're gonna be best friends or anything, but I guess I can tolerate you."

"I'm flattered," I said ironically. "All my life, I wanted to be tolerable."

"It's not much of a goal, but congratulations on reaching it," he deadpanned.

"Thanks, I think." I frowned at him and shook my head. Calling a truce with him was a relief. I hoped we could make it last. For all of our sakes.

Chapter Twenty-Four

Chelsea

Sadie's eyes widened. "So there's a new coach now?"

"Any day now." I sipped my coffee and nodded. "Coach Stanley's remains were found in his car, just off the highway. He hit a tree and it burst into flames, incinerating him and the car."

"Holy shit," she whispered. "That's terrible."

"It is." I couldn't quite meet her eyes. "They're starting to say the Smashers are cursed or something. First it was the GM, now the head coach."

"I'm sure it's a coincidence," she hedged. "Let's hope the whole 'things happen in threes' thing doesn't happen here. Who knows who might be next?"

I had a fair idea of a couple of people who were

in the firing line, but I didn't want to involve her any more than was absolutely necessary. Knowing Sadie, she'd want to jump right in with the rest of us. I didn't want to put her in that position. The web was tangled enough as it was.

"It's just one of those things," I said. "Curses aren't real."

"Are you sure about that?" She gave me the side eye. "Maybe you should get some sage and do whatever it is they do to cleanse the stadium or evil spirits." She waved her hand in the air like she was doing just that.

I snorted softly. "You know we're in Dusk Bay, right? If we tried to cleanse the place of evil spirits, there might not be anyone left."

She giggled. "We'd be left. And I'm sure all of those guys of yours would be left. Maybe a handful of other people. At least we wouldn't have to wait in line to buy an ice cream."

"That's Sadie, always with her priorities in place," I teased. "What could be more important than ice cream?"

"Exactly," she said. "And we could move into one of those huge mansions on the cliff. Who could stop us?"

"The fact we don't want to be squatters?" I suggested.

"We wouldn't be," she said. "If everyone disappeared, the property values would be down the toilet. We could pick one up for a steal."

"You thought this through, haven't you?" I asked. "Suddenly, it wouldn't surprise me if you had shares in a sage farm."

"I like to be very sage," she deadpanned.

I snorted. "With jokes like that, you might sage yourself away."

She grinned. "Absolutely not. I'm as sweet as—" She leaned over to grab a packet of sugar from the bowl on the table.

A crack echoed through the morning air, followed by a spray of blood.

It took a fraction of a second for me to realise the sound was a gunshot before I was grabbing for her and dragging us both down to the ground.

Thank you for reading! The story continues in Dirty Ruck. If you'd love a steamy bonus scene from Atlas' point of view, you can find it here.

About the Author

Maggie Alabaster writes reverse harem romance.

She lives in NSW, Australia with one spouse, two daughters, one dog, and countless birds.

Sign up for Maggie's newsletter! Sign Up!

Join Maggie's reader group! Join here!

Follow Maggie on Bookbub! Click here to follow me!

Check out Maggie's website- www.maggiealabaster.com

Also by Maggie Alabaster

Ruck Boys

Filthy Ruck

Hard Ruck

Twisted Ruck

Bad Ruck

Dirty Ruck

Deadly Ruck

Sparrow and the Mafia Kings

Possessive

Ruined

Corrupted

Pucking Dark Hearts

Pucking Hearts Collide

Pucking Forbidden Hearts

Pucking Hardened Hearts

Dusk Bay Demons

Puck Drop

Breakaway

Power Play

Brutal Academy

Book 1 Heartless

Book 2 Cruel

Book 3 Vengeful

Court of Blood and Binding

Book 1 Song of Scent and Magic

Book 2 Crown of Mist and Heat

Book 3 Sword of Balm and Shadow

Book 4 Whisper of Frost and Flame

Dark Masque

Book 1 Bait

Book 2 Prey

Book 3 Trap

Saving Abbie

Book 1 Pitch

Book 2 Pound

Book 3 Session

Book 4 Muse

Book 5 Rhythm

Book 6 Encore

Novella Venomous

Saving Abbie books 1-4

Saving Abbie books 4-6 + Venomous

Ruthless Claws

Book 1 Ivory

Book 2 Crimson

Book 3 Elodie

Harmony's Magic

Book 1 Summoned by Fire

Book 2 Summoned by Fate

Book 3 Summoned by Desire

Shifter's Vault

Book 1 Discarded

Book 2 Deceived

Book 3 Disgraced

My Alien Mates

Book 1 Star Warriors

Book 2 Star Defenders

Book 3 Star Protectors

Academy of Modern Magic

Book 1 Digital Magic

Book 2 Virtual Magic

Book 3 Logical Magic

Complete Collection

Summer's Harem

Book 1: Shimmer

Book 2: Glimmer

Book 3: Flicker

Complete collection

Short reads

Taken by the Snowmen

Jingle All the Way

Also by Maggie Alabaster and Erin Yoshikawa

Caught by the Tide

Book 1–Pursued by Shadows

Book 2 Pursued by Darkness

Book 3 Pursued by Monsters